I0586254

TRUE IDENTITY

Michelle Larmer

Copyright © 2022 MPA Publishing

All rights reserved, including the right to
reproduce this book, or portions thereof, in any
form without written permission except for the
use of brief quotations embodied in critical
articles and reviews.

This is a work of fiction. Names, characters,
places and incidents are either the product of
the author's imagination or are used fictitiously,
and any resemblance to actual persons, living or
dead, business establishments, events or locales
is entirely coincidental.

Published by MPA Publishing
Paperback ISBN: 978-0-6453083-2-7
Cover Design by Stuart Eadie
Edited by The Editing Pen

For my sister, Christina who inspires me to write
novels and who mentors me every step of the way.
Thank you.

PROLOGUE

There was no air.
Breathing was impossible, and panic set in.
She tried to calm her desperate fear and think, but it was impossible.
The awfulness of her situation was too great.

CHAPTER 1: ANNE-MARIE
Sunday 5 November

'Are we there yet?' Anne-Marie said, mimicking the voice of an impatient child, and earned a round of giggles from her two besties, as anticipated.

Anne-Marie had organised the Mount Kosciusko walk to celebrate turning fifty and couldn't imagine a better way to mark the slightly daunting milestone than being here with Nina and Louise.

Anne-Marie was the oldest—and the most adventurous—when it came to outdoor endeavours. Kayaking, canyoning, ziplining, abseiling… she loved it all. She knew that when the time came, Louise would be celebrating her big five-oh at a chef's table at a three-hatted restaurant, and Nina would insist on them luxuriating at a spa weekend. They were each very different in that respect, yet a friendship of more than twenty-five years had bound them together.

The trio had set off half an hour earlier from the drop-off point at the Thredbo chairlift, opting to avoid hiking the four-kilometre steep ascent from the village. So far, the track had been easy walking along an elevated metal platform erected to protect the fragile terrain, some of which was still covered in snow stubbornly clinging. In other parts, wildflowers bloomed in patches of rich brown earth.

'Come on, girls! Put your back into it!' Nina fired off the command, impersonating a drill sergeant as she marched past in exaggerated strides, her metal poles swinging through the air.

More laughter ensued as they slowly walked towards the summit of Mount Kosciusko.

Summer might have officially started, but the alpine region was largely oblivious. A late snowfall last month had left evidence of white cover across the mountain. A cross-country skier was visible in the distance, and a couple of diehard snowboarders were far above, embracing the extended season.

'It's glorious!' Louise shouted, stopping to fiddle with the complicated dials on her new Canon camera to capture the view of Australia's highest peak. 'Come on, guys, let me take one of you with the mountain range behind.'

Anne-Marie and Nina hugged in close and put their walking poles in front for an action pose, but they needn't have rushed. Louise took ages taking the photo, adjusting the zoom and resolution intently. No quick iPhone clicks for her.

The air was a crisp ten degrees, and the bright sunshine made for ideal walking conditions. The track was well maintained, and they had it largely to themselves. Almost. Further along, Anne-Marie could see a pair of hikers who were determined to break a land speed record in their quest to the top. Never stopping or slowing down to take in the splendour.

As Anne-Marie and her friends walked higher, the air began to whistle around them.

Louise and her Canon again slowed the walking party down, but Anne-Marie didn't mind. It gave her a chance to discreetly check her messages again. No, still nothing. But she wouldn't let it bother her; she was here in this glorious wilderness with her two closest friends. Anne-Marie slipped her phone back inside her jacket and drank thirstily from her water bottle, watching a lone skier traverse the mountainside.

The stark figure swayed from left to right in exaggerated movements, maintaining momentum as they carved a fluid passage through the snow. It looked like hard work, and she wondered if they would run out of ground cover before long. Just below was evidence of summer winning the battle of the seasons with more earth, grass and flowers visible. Soon all the mountain would look like that—removed of her protective white coat. Exposed. Vulnerable.

Anne-Marie suddenly squinted as something caught her attention where the snow met the barren brown earth.

'What's that, Lou? Over there. Can you zoom in?'

Louise immediately swerved her camera to where Anne-Marie was pointing and adjusted the lens. 'It's something blue?' Louise replied puzzled, showing Anne-Marie the image on her small digital screen.

'How do you make it larger?'

Louise took another round of photos, increasing the zoom function on each. 'Maybe plastic or it could be… It looks like something blue… clothing? A ski jacket? You can't really tell.'

'Let's take a closer look,' Anne-Marie said, moving off the track.

'Don't we have to stay on the path? Preserve the pristine environment or whatever the walking notes said?' Nina protested. 'Plus it looks really slippery.'

'No, come on. We'll zigzag over on the dirt parts,' Anne-Marie said determinedly, striding away.

The others were slow to respond, but Anne-Marie knew they would follow and kept up a brisk pace.

Getting closer, she squinted at the blue item. It looked like denim jeans.

Almost reaching the spot, she suddenly halted.

There was no doubt. It was definitely denim.

The sleeve of a denim jacket.

Putting her hand up to stop Nina and Louise from coming any closer, she gulped back a wave of nausea rising up her throat. Her heart began to race as she realised what she was looking at.

A slender wrist and long pale fingers fanned out from the sleeve. A dainty silver wristwatch at odds with the horrific scene.

'My God!' Louise's voice startled Anne-Marie, who hadn't expected her to appear beside her so suddenly.

'Shit! Shit! SHIT!' Louise repeated, as Nina put her hands over her mouth and crouched down on her heels, looking faint. Like she might throw up.

They huddled together, looking at what was now impossible to unsee.

CHAPTER 2: ANNE-MARIE

Fluorescent vests illuminated the mountain as an army of police, National Parks and Wildlife Service officers and other official-looking personnel swamped the scene.

Anne-Marie, Louise and Nina were sitting back at the walkway, which had now been closed off for the day—preventing any more foot traffic from passing through the otherwise pristine wilderness. A young park ranger stood a little distance down the path, redirecting curious trekkers back.

'We'll need to speak with you, so please wait,' a local policewoman had instructed them over an hour ago, and Anne-Marie was now feeling irritable. And she wasn't alone.

'Why can't we just head back to the chalet? Surely they can speak to us there?' pleaded Nina, getting up to stretch, moving gracefully into her regular yoga poses.

'Maybe they need us to show them—you know— walk them through what we did? How we found it... I mean *her*...,' Louise suggested, looking unsure.

'I guess... I'm just getting so cold.' Nina bent down from her waist, wrapping her arms around her calves, continuing to move and extend her body in languid movements.

'I'll see what's going on,' Anne-Marie announced, spotting the female Jindabyne cop they had spoken to earlier. The young officer was standing just inside the police tape, talking with a couple of other officers.

As Anne-Marie walked closer to the cordoned-off area, the air crackled with activity as orange vests industriously moved around the scene of their grim discovery. It didn't look like they had done much to uncover the woman's body in the past hour, and Anne-Marie was relieved to not be confronted by more than she could cope with.

Sensing her presence, a couple of lairy vests turned in her direction, and Anne-Marie could see the policewoman was now on the phone. Recognising Anne-Marie, the officer held up a finger to signal *wait*, before ending her call and walking over to meet her.

'Sorry to interrupt. We just wanted to know if we could go back to Thredbo and wait there?' Anne-Marie asked, now feeling foolish as the policewoman and the others watched on. There was a dead woman buried in the snow, and they wanted to go back to their nice warm apartment. How small-minded and selfish that must sound. Anne-Marie grimaced apologetically.

'If you don't mind waiting,' the officer said, smiling kindly. 'I was just on the line with the Queanbeyan detective, and he's about ten minutes away. He'll want to talk to you up here. The parks guys have set up some water, coffee and tea, so why don't I come with you, and we'll pour a few hot drinks to take over to your friends?'

Anne-Marie and the officer moved away from the scene towards a small makeshift camp set up with four chairs and two fold-up tables containing an assortment of maps and several two-way radios, which occasionally burst into noise with echoey voices. To the side were a few thermoses and large bottles of fresh drinking water with paper cups and sachets of sugar and milk.

Preparing the teas and accepting a few twin packs of Arnott's cream biscuits, Anne-Marie and the policewoman walked back to the pathway to deliver the beverages.

'Guys, this is Constable Jen Dillon. She's kindly offered us some hot drinks. Apparently, it won't be too much longer,' Anne-Marie said, handing over the teas to Louise and Nina.

'Actually, that sounds like them now,' Constable Dillon said, glancing up at the sky.

They all looked up, now noticing the engine noise and a black helicopter spinning towards them. After a few minutes, the chopper hovered over a flat part of the terrain about three hundred metres away and carefully lowered to the ground.

Two men leapt out, scurrying away from the roaring rotor blades towards the site, and Anne-Marie and the others returned their gaze to watch the chopper lift to the sky and disappear in the direction it had come.

'I'd better go over.' There was a nervous edge to the constable's voice, and Anne-Marie sensed a hierarchy had now been established. Their importance seemed to scream as loudly as the machine they'd arrived in. The two men had instantly commanded everyone's full attention.

Constable Dillon dashed over to greet the men, stopping halfway to call back to them. 'I'll update you ladies on the timing soon. I promise!'

CHAPTER 3: MATTHEW

As Matthew strode towards the waiting throng, he took in the surrounds, gauging potential access routes.

The north side was incredibly steep before it plateaued to rise up again sharply, so it would present physical challenges but perhaps not to a capable skier or mountain climber in good ground cover. Opposite, the south was flatter, more manageable to traverse but very open and exposed. The west looked the most likely. A small forest about fifty metres away could provide clues. He would need a map to know what that woodland concealed. Where it led.

Reaching the police tape, Matthew automatically ducked under and then paused to hold it up so his colleague, Reginald Reynor, could slip through. Reynor had mentioned a recent hip replacement, and Matthew guessed the tricky terrain would be punishing on his new joint. However it was his expertise Matthew was after. Reynor had recently returned from an educational rotation with the crime scene unit in Sydney and was their best forensics investigator.

A young policewoman stood before them, holding out her hand.

'Hello, Detective and Senior Sergeant. I'm Constable Jenny Dillon from Jindabyne, and this is National Parks and Wildlife head ranger, Guy Swan.'

'Matthew Calucci,' he said, shaking their hands.

'Good morning, or should I say *good afternoon*,' Sergeant Reynor said somewhat formally with a nod to both. 'May I?' Reynor indicated the snow-covered mound, not waiting for permission before marching over, followed quickly by the others.

A bubbling commentary ensued from the young officer, eager to impart everything she knew.

Matthew had already heard the details—scant as they were—over the phone earlier, but he was reluctant to stop her. Plus it was useful to hear the repetition in context.

Looking down, he saw a woman's hand reaching out of the snow. Translucent skin, unblemished and slender in form. A denim sleeve concealed her arm, much of which, together with her body, was still hidden under snow. Icy crystals appeared in spots where the snow must have once been thick and continued to cling in patches, despite the mild temperatures. Nothing appeared to be disturbed, a miracle when there were so many people moving about the site. This would assist the investigation enormously.

Crouching down beside Reynor, Matthew watched as he inserted his thermometer and other instruments, carefully recording details.

The slow, methodical process prompted Matthew to get back to his feet. He knew from experience that Reynor wouldn't say much until his tests had been completed.

He moved around the motionless figure, looking back up the ridge and down the slope, continuing to puzzle over the location.

'Can you get me some maps of the area?'

'Sure, I'll grab them now.' The ranger moved away, anxious to be of use.

'We've taken plenty of photos and videos,' the constable offered eagerly. 'We didn't want to extricate before you'd examined the scene.'

'Quite right,' said Reynor in stern approval. 'We will get started now if that works for you, Matthew?'

Nodding, Matthew moved back and allowed space for two enlisted volunteers to aid Reynor's work.

Reynor held up his hand to signal the others to wait and began to gently carve out the ice on the woman's hand and cuff of the jacket before inching his way along the sleeve towards her shoulder. Occasionally he stopped to make notes on his audio recorder and request photos before continuing.

Matthew was reluctant to leave but knew he should use the time to interview the first witnesses. Progress would be slow in extricating the victim, so he left them to it and followed the constable to the waiting group of women.

Offering to fetch him a black coffee, she left.

'Please, let's sit.' He motioned towards them.

'I need to stand. My bum's killing me,' snapped the brunette woman, sounding annoyed at being kept waiting. A nervous laughter went through the group.

Introducing himself, he asked for each of their names and addresses, noting them down in his small notebook.

'Anne-Marie Christenson, Double Bay, Sydney,' said the agitated woman.

'I'm Nina. Nina Simmons. I'm also from Sydney. Bronte,' she said nervously, hugging herself as if to keep warm or possibly calm down her nerves.

After a pause, he looked up to prompt the third woman.

'Umm. It's Louise Jorgen, but I was Louise Rodgers—you might remember me? From uni in Canberra?' she said, squinting at him before giving a warm smile.

Studying her, he could now see it. Of course. She'd filled out since their university days, but not much else had changed in the past thirty years. Her dimples were the giveaway and those striking blue eyes that seemed to dance with amusement, even now.

'Louise? Of course,' he said, surprised to reunite with her after all this time.

'Yeah. What are the chances, hey?' She went to laugh but suppressed it with a hand to her mouth. 'Sorry. That was bloody stupid. It's awful.' She grimaced, looking over at the scene.

'Yeah. It's that all right. Anyway, let's get this over with and leave the catch-up for later,' he said, giving her a reassuring nod and writing down her details.

For the next thirty minutes the women shared their account of discovering the woman's body.

'Something just didn't look right,' Anne-Marie said, taking the lead. 'That's why we zeroed in to see what was over there and then headed off the track to get a closer look.' She was clearly the group leader, and her friends let her tell the story.

'Is it that young snowboarder who went missing?' Louise asked, looking both hopeful and perplexed as if wondering if that was an appropriate thing to ask.

Sixteen-year-old Ella Williams had disappeared last winter whilst snowboarding at Thredbo with her family, and despite an extensive manhunt and media campaign, she had never been found.

Matthew also wanted that mystery to be solved but knew enough by now not to speak before all the evidence was in hand.

CHAPTER 4: MATTHEW

'My initial observations are that the deceased has been here for two days, possibly one or two more but certainly not longer than four,' pronounced Reynor when Matthew rejoined him.

Whilst there was no identification on her, both the time frame and the woman's age, which was estimated to be mid-twenties, ruled out the teenage snowboarder. There would undoubtedly be anxious messages from the Williams family, drawing the same mistaken conclusion that Matthew and Louise had hoped for. Would they be relieved? Or would the ongoing wait torment them even further?

'See here?' Reynor continued, indicating the woman's throat. 'Strangulation. No doubt about it. There are ligature marks and significant eye haemorrhaging.'

'Whether that was the fatal blow, we'll need full blood work and physical findings from the autopsy,' Reynor concluded, packing up his kit.

'Okay, so we've got a twenty-something female. We'll need to check the missing persons first. Any distinguishing features?'

'None that I've yet ascertained, I'm afraid,' said Reynor. 'But let's see what the physical examination brings forth.'

The helicopter was back and waiting to transport Reynor and the deceased, and in minutes it had lifted away.

Matthew didn't plan on returning to Queanbeyan immediately. There was more to be gained by investigating the scene for clues, as well as talking to locals and the park rangers. Someone must have seen something.

A thorough search of the area was underway and would go into the night and tomorrow. Door-knocking teams would be in place in the morning, although he wasn't overly confident. The off season had reduced the population in Thredbo considerably to keen trekkers and desperate skiers getting their last fix for the year.

Less than five percent of the chalets were occupied, according to the National Parks and Wildlife Service team he'd spoken to. And of the seventy or so businesses in town, the local pub, two restaurants, one café and an adventure hire shop were all that remained open this late in the season. When the snow season ended, the exodus left a ghost town in its wake.

Matthew would scour the maps and access routes this evening before meeting the head ranger in the morning for a more thorough investigation. He wanted to take a fresh look and gain a greater sense of the place.

But all that could wait. Right now there was an old friend he intended to meet for a much-overdue drink.

CHAPTER 5: ANNE-MARIE

She was pissed off that they had spent half the day, waiting around for a Queanbeyan detective to arrive, only to repeat everything she'd already said to the more than competent Jindabyne police hours earlier. Because of the hold-up, she had missed a call from Henry. So bloody frustrating.

Anne-Marie stormed upstairs to her room in the chalet. She was well aware that her girlfriends would have noticed her dark mood, but she didn't care. This was meant to be her special birthday weekend. Plus bloody Louise was going out for a drink with *him*!

'I hope you don't mind?' Louise had murmured as they entered the apartment twenty minutes earlier.

What could she say? 'No, you're supposed to be having drinks with *me*! I'm the birthday girl, remember?'

That would have sounded so juvenile. But then again, so was stomping around upstairs. But tough luck!

Anne-Marie had been hibernating for the past half an hour and tried in vain to reach Henry, but of course it went to voicemail. Her calls to Henry *always* went to voicemail.

Henry was incredibly busy, she knew that. His whirlwind lifestyle filled with endless business meetings and social engagements had been a big part of his appeal. He led a glamorously successful life, and she was prepared to wait it out because soon enough it would be hers too. It was the type of lifestyle she had always envisaged for herself. A luxury home in Perth, a diary filled with social soirées and never having to worry about money ever again. Henry had promised her the world. She just had to be patient.

That thought buoyed her spirits as she moved into the en suite to run a bath. A gift set of lavender salts and scented candle sat by the sink, and she poured the salts liberally, swishing them around in the warm, flowing water. Lighting the candle, she stripped off her walking clothes and lowered herself into the tub.

The water was like a soothing balm to her stiff muscles and sour mood. Her lower back ached from sitting on that uncomfortable walkway for hours on end. She closed her eyes and let the water continue to rise over her body, up to her chest before using her big toe to nudge off the tap.

Resting her head back on a folded towel, she closed her eyes and breathed in and out slowly to release the tension and disappointment of the day.

But then the awfulness of the day hit her, and her eyes flew wide open. A woman was dead. Buried in the snow at Mount Kosciusko. An ice-cold shiver went through her, and she felt a wave of guilt at her petty behaviour.

She nudged the hot water back on, wanting to get rid of the chill.

That poor woman would never celebrate another birthday, let alone another day, with friends or family.

It was truly awful to think that they had been just a few metres from a dead person.

She vowed to be kinder and more compassionate and stop resenting everyone around her, including the useless police guys, Louise for abandoning her tonight, and even Henry for being so bloody unreachable!

There would be plenty of time for her to enjoy the fruits of life. She just needed to stop worrying.

CHAPTER 6: MATTHEW

Matthew was on his mobile when Louise arrived, and he waved her over.

She hadn't aged at all, he thought, watching her casually stroll across the room to the table. Hard to believe it had been decades since they had last caught up, and yet he would have recognised her instantly now that her hair was loose, released from the baseball cap she had been wearing on the mountain this afternoon. Her blond-streaked hair was longer than she'd worn it at university, but the extra length suited her. It made her look girlish and carefree. Her colourful, dangly earrings and bohemian scarf wrapped snugly around her neck were also giveaways, her signature look even back then.

'Sorry,' he mouthed, but she shook her head and indicated she would head to the bar and get a drink. When he signalled he was right with his beer, she walked away.

'Leslie, I'll wrap up now. If nothing turns up, get Robbo to check interstate, okay? Cheers,' he said, ending the call. The identity of their victim was still a mystery, but he hoped it wouldn't be for too much longer.

Putting his phone face down on the table, he took a slug of his beer, as Louise returned, holding a large glass of red wine and a packet of potato crisps.

'I figured you probably haven't eaten for a few hours?' she said, her smile revealing those cute dimples that had all the guys crazy back in the day.

'You look great, Louise,' he said. 'Why haven't you got old like the rest of us?'

'You big charmer!' She laughed dismissively, rolling her eyes. 'You clearly haven't changed either. Still one for the flattery.'

Ripping open the bag of chips, Louise took a few before sliding the packet towards him. 'What a weird day hey?'

'Yeah,' he agreed. 'Thanks for coming out. I'm sure you and your friends are shattered by the whole thing.'

It was different for him. He was familiar with death, and whilst it would always affect him, he had learnt over the years how to compartmentalise scenes like today. Matthew approached crime like a puzzle, moving pieces into place to create a clearer picture of what he was dealing with. Only then would his mind begin the process of methodically sorting the information and narrowing the search for the perpetrators. But for Louise, today's discovery would have been a huge shock and one that was no doubt still reverberating.

'How are you feeling?' he asked. 'Do you want to talk about it?'

'No,' she said after a pause. 'Let's talk about something more uplifting, maybe what you've done since leaving ANU?'

'Sure. Well as you can see, I ended up in the police force.'

'I noticed.' Louise laughed. 'I thought you were going to be a hotshot lawyer? All those bloody Tortes lectures we went to.' Her face grimaced at the memory they both shared of those torturous hours of listening to a boring lecturer prattle on and on.

'I actually started down that path at Stewarts, Bright and Collier in Sydney but hated it for the first few years, until I moved into criminal law. After about five years I decided I was done with the bullshit and billable hours of working up defences for guilty clients and felt I'd make a greater contribution by getting out from behind the desk and into the coalface. So off to the Academy, first stop Bathurst, then Wagga and south again to Queanbeyan. I've been a detective now for seven years and get a lot of satisfaction from it. Sure, the hours are crap, so too the pay.' He smirked. 'But it's "real", you know? I'm not just sitting in a gilded office, representing those who can afford it.'

Louise got it. He saw it in the way her eyes lit up. There was a knowing in that look.

'Do you catch up with any of the old gang?' She reached for a handful of chips.

A pang of guilt moved through him, because he could have made more effort over the years, especially with good friends like Louise. If he had only known that she too had ended up settling in Canberra.

'I did when I was in Sydney working with Stewarts, but even then, the hours were crazy, and I just didn't seem to have time. Then when I went into the police, my life became even less of my own. This job is all-encompassing and doesn't leave much room for anything else. We're pretty crap at our personal lives.'

'Speaking of which?' She lifted her eyes, rounded playfully, her cute dimples returning.

'What?' he said, trying to sound vague although they both knew what she was referring to.

'Marriage? Kids? Kelly?' she asked, each word punctuated with curiosity.

'No, no and no,' he said, taking a gulp and sitting back, shaking his head.

'Oh? We all thought you and Kelly were the real deal.'

'Yeah, but then the big wide world opened up and Kelly headed to New York, and I went off to Sydney, met Monica and got married, then divorced. No kids, but probably for the best, hey?' His smile was half-hearted, and Louise reached out to squeeze his arm.

'What about you, though? What have you been doing for the past twenty-five years?'

'I'm married and have a beautiful daughter.' Louise's eyes brimmed with love, and she began to fill him in on her life.

CHAPTER 7: LOUISE

Theodore Edward Bartholomew Jorgen was every inch his name. Never a simple *Theo*, not even as a child and certainly never in all the time that Louise had been with him. There was an old-fashioned formality about Theodore that had attracted her from the start. He was so completely different to her past boyfriends, eschewing the skinny black jeans and moody attitude for a three-piece suit and a leather satchel, which he continued to wear across his now portly frame as he left for work each morning.

He had been the exact opposite of Rex, the one who had broken her heart again and again with his flirtatious charm and too-frequent one-night flings as he and the Thunders toured the country and abroad. Her heart fractured a little more each time she learnt of another of Rex's betrayals, but what could she do? He was the lead singer of Melbourne's hottest rock band, and it was the price she paid for being part of his rock 'n' roll lifestyle. But when she hit thirty-one, she knew it was time to move on from the seedy pubs and dingy music venues and find someone for the long game. Someone to have children with. Build a life with. And then she met Theodore.

Twelve months later she had Chloe, a terrace in Canberra and a sizable diamond on her finger. For that, she would always indulge Theodore's eccentricities, odd peculiarities and outdated snobbery. Sure, she might whinge from time to time because he was set in his ways, but he was her life partner, and without him she would never feel complete nor have Chloe. The love of their life.

Now the only slight fly in the ointment was that Chloe had moved out of home and Louise felt bereft and lonely without her. But at least Louise had her jewellery business. It was an enormous source of creative pleasure as well as a going concern.

Louise's studio in Canberra's trendy Kingston was now an institution among the fashion set, and since Chloe's departure to a shared house and a gap year and Theodore's increasingly singular pursuits of composing symphonies, it had become her haven, her sanctuary.

Without New Age Jewels, her life would be missing its purpose. Was that how Anne-Marie felt? Was that why she'd pursued this ridiculous relationship without heeding the warning signs?

CHAPTER 8: ANNE-MARIE
Monday 6 November

WOMAN FOUND IN ICY GRAVE silently screamed News.com.au, whilst the *Sydney Morning Herald* adopted a more sober story halfway down the home page: KOSCIUSKO TREKKERS DISCOVER BODY.

Eagerly reading the stories on her laptop on the sofa, Anne-Marie sipped her milky tea and nibbled on the vegemite toast she had just made.

The detective friend of Louise's featured a bit in the quotes, in which he managed to say very little, and the photos accompanying the copy. One was a file shot of him looking very dapper with a clean shave and confident smile, and the other picture was taken from the site yesterday. He looked serious, grim and intense in a semicircle of other police and National Parks volunteers. She recognised a few of the faces.

'Happy birthday, love,' Louise said, as she padded into the lounge room, wearing a matching hotel-issue white dressing gown.

'Oh, thanks, Lou.' They exchanged a hug as Louise curled up beside her.

'What are you looking at?' Louise asked, peering over at the screen.

'I just wanted to see if there were any developments from yesterday. Your dishy detective gets quite a splash,' Anne-Marie said, turning her laptop to show the close-up photo of Matthew speaking with the troops. 'Any more *dates* for you and the delectable detective?'

'He's just an old uni mate.' Louise waved off her stirring and concentrated on reading the story. 'It doesn't say anything about identifying the woman?' Louise sounded disappointed.

'I know. In fact, there's not much in there that we don't already know.'

'Oooh, I love how they mention us as three female trekkers.' Louise giggled.

'More like plodders!' said Anne-Marie, and they hooted with laughter.

Just then a message box popped up alerting Anne-Marie to an incoming email, and she realised it was *him*. Finally!

'Oh, I need to get this. It's Henry!' She jumped up urgently. 'I'll take this upstairs.' Anne-Marie hurried away, clutching her laptop, desperate to connect with her beautiful beau.

'Sure, love. After, shall we go out and get some coffee? Nins is in the shower, so just give us a hoy when you're ready?' Louise's voice faded as Anne-Marie almost ran to her room. She did not want to miss this precious window with Henry.

However her efforts were futile. By the time she had shut the bedroom door and opened up his message, she found just a few simple words waiting for her.

My darling, miss you like crazy. Meetings all day. xx

PS How about a sexy photo to keep me going until we talk?
Xxxxxxxxxxx

Disappointed he hadn't rung her for her birthday, she sank back on the bed and reread the message. It had been over a week now since they had talked on the phone, and she missed his voice. She hadn't been able to convince him to use Zoom, FaceTime, Skype or any other video means of connecting.

'I'm old school like that,' he had remonstrated, instead suggesting they send a photo with each email. And those photos that had started off innocently enough—Anne-Marie posing in her cycling gear about to head off with her Sunday morning crew, Henry lifting a martini glass at a dimly lit New York wine bar—had progressively turned raunchier, as had their phone calls. She had never had phone sex before Henry and was finding it a poor substitute for the real thing.

Slipping off her robe and sliding her silk nightdress down, she posed provocatively at her phone camera, attempting to look seductive and confident. After clicking about half a dozen times, she slipped her nightie back into place and scanned the images, choosing one that didn't make her look ridiculous and would command his full attention.

****

Half an hour later, Anne-Marie, Nina and Louise walked into the View café, which was heaving with people. Almost every laminate table was full, and the chatter of conversation loud and faintly competitive. Phones were pressed to the ears of some, whilst others paused their conversation and glanced in their direction, as if hoping to find someone worth interviewing. There were men in sharp suits and women in heels, both looking out of place in the casual diner but who would be picture perfect during their live TV crosses to the masses later on.

'Journos,' explained the harried proprietor, who only the day before had been hard for them to shake off in his desperate need for company and conversation.

'They just keep arriving! Reporters from Sydney, Canberra, everywhere!' He shook his head, in awe at the turn of events, before hastily returning his gaze to them. 'You've heard the news?'

'You mean the woman?' Louise asked, and the man nodded.

'Actually, we were the ones who—' Nina began, before Anne-Marie abruptly cut her off.

'Let's get the orders in, girls! It's busy so we'd best keep things moving,' urged Anne-Marie, giving Nina a steely glance before proceeding to order. Anne-Marie didn't want to become part of the media circus and wasn't about to volunteer them as fodder for the hungry pack. It was beneath them, she thought.

'Sure, ladies,' he said, unperturbed, noting down their breakfast orders.

'My turn to fix this up,' Nina offered, swiping her platinum AMEX card.

'Sorry, love, that card is declined,' the proprietor said sympathetically.

'What? No, it's fine. Try again please.'

'Why don't I pay?' Louise proposed, but Nina shook her head.

'It's fine. It will just be the internet connection.'

'Still not working, love. Have you got another card?'

'Here, please use mine.' Louise thrust her credit card over as the queue behind them shuffled impatiently.

'Yeah, all sorted,' the proprietor said cheerily, handing over the receipt as the girls moved to the last vacant table.

'Thanks, Lou. I don't know why it's not working,' Nina murmured.

'Oh, love, it's probably a security thing. Maybe just let the bank know you're out of town in case they've frozen it,' Louise suggested, before recounting a trip to Prague when she'd failed to notify her bank and couldn't use her card for the entire trip.

Anne-Marie wasn't really listening, her mind returning to Henry and trying to work out what was niggling her... There was something, but she couldn't work out what. But then a catch in Nina's voice made her return her focus back to the table.

'A bank security stuff up. Or maybe even a scam?' Nina's words didn't sound quite as convincing as they should, her pitch too high and her attempt to dismiss the glitch a little uncertain.

What am I missing? Anne-Marie wondered.

CHAPTER 9: MATTHEW

The police had set up a temporary headquarters at the Pioneers Pub in Thredbo's main street, equipping the small function room upstairs with half a dozen tables and chairs, as well as laptops, a large whiteboard and several phones. A picture window faced Thredbo Mountain and the now stationary chairlift, which cut a severe line down the centre of it.

Matthew had briefed the Jindabyne and Cooma police teams before they had set off to door knock local businesses and lodges in the hope that someone saw something.

On one of the makeshift desks, three National Parks officers were reviewing maps and plotting the various access routes to look at.

'Here you go,' said Constable Jen Dillon, placing a black coffee in front of Matthew and sliding over a muffin.

'The muffins are the best in Jindabyne, and the coffee is the best I can do from downstairs.'

'Thanks,' Matthew said, picking up the coffee. 'Any word?'

'Not yet. The team debrief is at midday, but they'll call if they discover anything earlier.'

Nodding, Matthew bit into the muffin. The berries provided a delicious jolt of sweetness and acidity to the bitter coffee that he was persevering with.

Before he could comment, his phone rang.

'Matthew Calucci.'

'Good morning, Detective, it's Senior Constable Wales from Sydney. I have an identity for you.'

'I'll put you on speaker,' Matthew said, switching on the function before reaching for a notepad and pen. 'Go ahead. I've got Constable Dillon with me from Jindabyne.'

'I'll email this through, but we believe the woman is Madeline Bright. A twenty-eight-year-old Surry Hills resident. She was reported missing an hour ago.'

'An hour ago? That's strange. Reynor believes she's been up here for a few days.'

'Homicide detectives are arranging to talk to her flatmates, boyfriend, employer… all the usuals to paint a picture of last movements. All we can say for certain is that her photograph is a match with the Jane Doe in the morgue. We're arranging a positive ID now.'

'Who reported her missing?' he asked.

'One of her flatmates. Lizzie Riggs.'

'Right.'

'We'll get the positive ID established in the next few hours when the flatmate does the formal ID, and I'll notify you when that's done.'

'Thanks. Keep us posted and send what you have through on my email now.'

After ending the call, he sat back in his chair and noticed that the National Parks guys had paused their map reading to look over.

'How does a Surry Hills woman end up here?' Matthew posed the question to the full room, before turning to stare out at the mountain range.

'How come she was only reported missing this morning?' Constable Jen Dillon replied with the next most compelling question.

How indeed, he thought, taking a gulp of his bitter coffee, which had turned horribly cold.

CHAPTER 10: NINA

Nina was worried. Very worried. Her credit card had been frozen. But why? The conversation with the bank's customer service manager was less than satisfactory, telling her what she already knew. She couldn't use her credit card. Durgh!

What she didn't understand was *why*? Before she could dispute the two recent large transactions on her account, which equated to a staggering $22,000, she would need to speak with David. He might know something. Or perhaps her card had been scammed? Yes! That must be it. Her husband rarely used her credit card; he had plenty of his own. But then again David spent his life moving money around their various accounts, so she would need to check with him first before escalating the matter with the bank's fraud team.

Phoning David's number again, she left a second voicemail. This time dispensing with the niceties. If her husband was transferring money without telling her, she would be livid.

'David, there's an issue with my credit card, and I need to sort it ASAP. Would you call me as soon as you get this message?' Ending the call, she paced the room, trying to calm her unsteady nerves.

Since marrying David eight years ago, he had been advising her on the financial side of her business. One of the *perks* of being married to a financial adviser, he had touted on more than a few occasions. Even her conservative accountant had had to concede that some of David's strategies had paid big dividends into her boutique talent agency, transforming it from a small to a medium player. The complicated investments had given her the capital to open a second office in Melbourne and then a third in Brisbane. She had signed on some larger accounts and secured highly sought-after models and actors, giving Talent Time both stature and profile in a competitive industry.

David would know what the problem was and have a solution, she reassured herself.

But still the phone didn't ring.

Nina finally stopped pacing and slumped down onto the carpet. Crossing her legs and sitting up tall, she tried the meditative breathing technique she had learnt and used many times over the years. Inhale for four breaths, hold for eight breaths, slowly release for eight breaths.

Just focus on the breath, Nina. Just focus on the breath.

CHAPTER 11: MATTHEW

The mountain looked innocently tranquil, dappled in gentle morning sunshine as Matthew walked along the walking track. Blinding white snow, piercing blue sky and unadulterated mountain air entered his lungs as he strode alongside head ranger Guy Swan. Today's postcard image of Mount Kosciusko was at odds with yesterday's grim discovery.

Matthew let his body feel at one with the environment and tried to tune into what the landscape was telling him. The mountainous terrain was forever changing as they followed the pathway upwards. Eventually he slipped back to follow in the ranger's footsteps, listening to his comfortable monotone voice explaining factual titbits on the various landmarks they passed.

They were close now, and Guy suddenly brought them to a halt.

'Yep, so…,' he said, pausing for a beat, 'we've identified three possible access routes to the scene. First, simply the way we've just come. But it's out in the open, long—about three kilometres.' He squinted into the distance.

'No. It's too far to carry someone… assuming she was carried in,' Matthew said dismissively. 'She certainly wasn't dressed for hiking.' The woman had been clothed in a light denim jacket, white pants and strappy flat sandals, hardly suitable for walking Kosciusko.

'The second option is over from the north,' Guy Swan said, pointing to a ridge. 'More challenging terrain but quicker overland and more concealed.'

'And the third option?'

'Over on the west.' The men turned their heads to the copse of trees in the distance.

'Flatter terrain, which is an advantage. And…' Guy was building up to something. Matthew could sense it in his more animated speech pattern. 'It's only about a kilometre to a fire trail.'

'What? You mean you can get vehicle access up this high?'

'Yep, too right. Hard to see it now with the winter snow still holding firm, but easy enough if you knew it was there, beyond the tree line.'

'What sort of vehicle would get up here?'

'All wheel, four wheel. Either would manage,' Guy said, shrugging. 'Of course, you'd need to know the way though because the trail hasn't been cleared yet for summer. I've got a crew over there now, checking for any sign of tyre treads. We are also sourcing a drone.'

'Good. Let's join them.'

As they walked over, they paused at the perimeter tape. Matthew studied the burial site for a few minutes, scanning for anything they might have missed yesterday. But all that remained was a lump of disturbed snow and dirt and a puddle of water where the grave had once been.

Guy's ringing phone interrupted Matthew's pondering.

Hanging up a few moments later, Guy announced, 'Yep, the guys have got something. You right to head over?'

'Let's go!' Matthew almost broke into a run towards the trees.

It didn't take long for the pair to cross the relatively flat plateau and reach the small forest. After walking through it for a short time, they came to the fire trail where Guy's team was waiting for them.

'Fresh tyre marks there and also over there,' one of the rangers said, pointing at a large area that had now been hastily taped off.

Crouching down, Matthew examined the markings and looked around. 'We'll need to get a team up here to check this out. Let's try to keep away from any obvious indicators so we don't stuff up the forensics.'

They all nodded.

Walking cautiously around the scene, he made his way back in the direction they had just come from and returned, trying to get a feel for the distance and possibility of someone walking this route, carrying a body. It was the most obvious scenario.

Suddenly something caught his eye, and he crouched down again. Sure enough, in front of him lay a discarded cigarette butt, more like a joint. Gingerly stepping back, he called for more markers so the forensic team would extract it without compromising the DNA profile, which could be significant.

CHAPTER 12: LOUISE

Anne-Marie and Nina seemed unusually subdued as they studied their menus, and Louise's attempts at conversation had fallen away. Neither of them had commented on the spectacular view of Mount Kosciusko from the window table she had organised for Anne-Marie's birthday lunch. Had they even noticed? Perhaps after the intense scrutiny of the food choices was over.

Louise had decided on the grilled octopus to start followed by the Asian fusion duck breast and sat back to ponder what was going on, both inside the heads of her two friends and outside. The chairlift continued to sit idle, and the mountain remained deserted. Matthew had mentioned that he'd be up there again today, and she wondered if he had discovered anything new.

Now looking around the restaurant, she watched the waiter attend to the only other table that was occupied. An older couple sat holding hands, talking quietly. She didn't hear what the waiter said, but their laughter carried through the restaurant and made her smile. The couple reluctantly released their hands as they made space for the bread basket and chatted amiably with the tall server as he replenished their wineglasses.

Bar Terrazo had been the only restaurant open on a Monday, and they had been lucky it was this one and not the more casual steakhouse. Anne-Marie loved fine dining, and the crisp white tablecloths, shiny parquetry floors and sophisticated open kitchen on the opposite side of the restaurant held great promise.

'Welcome, ladies. I'm Daniel, and I'll be looking after you today.' The waiter took his time to bestow a dazzling smile at each of them. 'May I take drink orders to start?'

'Shall we order a bottle of Prosecco? Toast the big birthday?' Louise proposed, determined to inject some energy into what was supposed to be a celebratory lunch after all.

'That sounds great.' Anne-Marie's face broke into a relieved half smile, and even Nina's pinched features released a fraction.

'It's Anne-Marie's birthday today,' Louise enthused to the suave waiter. 'And it's a significant one!' She was probably overdoing things, but she wanted the girls to zap out of their flat moods and remember why they were there. To have fun and enjoy Anne-Marie's fiftieth.

'Wonderful! Happy birthday, Anne-Marie.' He flashed a wolfish grin and winked in her direction, which seemed to do the trick in lightening her up.

Anne-Marie beamed with the attention.

'Let me organise your bottle, and I'll then take your food orders,' he said, gliding away from the table.

'Well, he's dishy?' Anne-Marie remarked as they watched him disappear behind the bar.

'Isn't he just! Now have you guys decided on your meals?' Louise asked, before sharing her selections from the menu.

They were still workshopping choices when Daniel returned to pop the Prosecco and pour the sparkling wine.

Toasting Anne-Marie, Louise couldn't help but notice that Nina had immediately gulped a decent amount of her wine. The lightest drinker of the three, her glass was nearly empty. Also noticing, Daniel topped it up instantly before moving away.

'Cheers!' they chorused, as Anne-Marie blew them each a kiss.

'How did you go with the bank?' Louise asked Nina after putting down her glass and reaching for some bread.

'Fine,' Nina said too quickly. 'David's sorting it out. So, what did your hunky businessman give you for your birthday?'

The change in topic was deliberate, but as it was Anne-Marie's day, Louise voiced her interest. 'Yes, how are things going with Mr Right?'

'Henry really wanted to be in town to spoil me, but he's just so busy, but we've got a luxury weekend planned for when I get back,' Anne-Marie gushed, now looking more relaxed and at ease.

'That's great!' Louise was relieved that Anne-Marie was finally going to have a face-to-face encounter with the mysterious Henry Dales.

'Is he coming over from Perth especially, or are you going over there?' Nina's excitement was also clear.

'He's coming to Sydney. Just to see me! How adorable is that? We're going to have two nights in the *penthouse* at the Langham Hotel. It's so decadent! And dinner at Tetsuya's.'

'Wow!' Nina exclaimed.

Louise was relieved to see the cloud hanging over Nina lift. But then watched as Nina reached to the ice bucket to refill her glass once more.

Anne-Marie seemed oblivious, instead radiating pure happiness and proudly expanding on what the magnificent Henry Dales had planned for her.

Louise truly hoped Anne-Marie wouldn't be let down... again. And wondered what the hell had got into Nina.

CHAPTER 13: MATTHEW

Unsurprisingly, the door-knock appeal had revealed very little, and Matthew now sat reading through Senior Constable Wales's emails. He was expecting two phone calls. The first, from the NSW Department of Forensic Medicine to confirm the woman's identity, which he suspected would be the newly missing Sydney woman, Madeline Bright.

Secondly, he was awaiting Reynor, who was en route to Thredbo. Together with a couple of officers, they would return to the mountain and inspect the tyre marks and surrounds for any other potentially useful evidence.

Matthew began to read the missing person report, which wasn't extensive. It stated that Maddy (as she was popularly known) had apparently last been seen on Friday, and as today was Monday, the timing fitted with Reynor's theory on the time of death.

According to the notes, the alarm bell was sounded at ten thirty this morning after the administration secretary at the school that Maddy worked at had rung her house to find out why she wasn't at work, nor answering her mobile. Lizzie Riggs, one of Maddy's three flatmates, had taken the call and telephoned around, eventually speaking to Maddy's boyfriend. The young man, Jake Smith, said that he hadn't seen Maddy since the previous Friday morning when she had stayed over at his place.

It transpired that Maddy hadn't arrived at work on Friday either, nor had she returned to her shared house over the weekend.

'How are you going?' Constable Dillon enquired, placing a Styrofoam cup of black coffee beside him.

'Just reading the missing person report, assuming this is our ID,' he said.

'Anything of interest?'

'The timing fits. The age fits. The circumstances are off. Madeline Bright has three housemates and a boyfriend, and yet she's only reported missing three days later,' he said, frowning at the constable, who he guessed was of a similar age.

'The flatmates thought she was at the boyfriend's all weekend, and vice versa?' she offered. 'What about family? My mother would be mental if I went AWOL for a few days without calling.'

'According to the file, she's an only child and her folks live in Singapore,' he answered.

After pondering the file for a few more minutes, his mobile rang, and he could see it was Reynor.

'Yes, it's Madeline Bright. The Sydney Lab just confirmed,' Reynor said, dispensing with any greetings.

They spoke for a few more minutes before agreeing to talk in more depth when Reynor arrived at the site in a few hours' time.

Matthew sat staring at the profile photo of Madeline Bright, looking so pretty and vibrant in her youth, and wondered what had happened for her life to be cut so cruelly short.

CHAPTER 14: ANNE-MARIE

Anne-Marie slumped on the bed, her body sagging with the effort of today's birthday lunch. Forcing a smile on her face and laughter in her voice had been exhausting, but she didn't want to admit to her best friends her disappointment in Henry. They had already given hints they didn't quite trust him, and she wasn't going to fuel their dislike further with her own misgivings.

Slowly undoing her drop pearl earrings, she placed them on the bedside table before unfastening her watch and sliding it, together with her trio of gold bracelets, off her wrist. She paused at the large emerald ring sitting on her ring finger on her right hand. The elaborately designed piece had been a three-month anniversary gift from Henry, and she momentarily felt guilty for doubting his affection. Surely he wouldn't lavish such an expensive piece of jewellery on her if he wasn't serious? But why couldn't he have given it to her today as a birthday gift? Or even just telephoned her? This morning's sexy photo swap now seemed cheap and belittling. Snatching off the ring, she dropped it on the bedside table with a clang and went into the bathroom to remove her make-up.

Minutes later her hair was up and the faucet rained warm water over her tight shoulders and back.

A luxury weekend at the Langham to spoil her for her birthday, yeah right. She didn't want to admit she had actually booked it all because Henry was "too busy". He had promised to fix her up when he came to Sydney.

'I can't have it on the company credit card, you see. I'll transfer the money from my personal account,' he had explained. She had also paid for his Perth business-class flight over for the same reason.

It would all be worth it though when he got here and they finally had two blissful days together. In the flesh.

By the time Anne-Marie switched off the shower, she felt revived, and after towelling herself off, dressed in jeans and a T-shirt and went to see what the girls were up to.

'I'm just worried she'll get hurt,' came Louise's voice.

Anne-Marie froze at the top of the stairs.

'Look, I agree. It's weird that she hasn't actually met him yet,' added Nina.

'Maybe he's a Nigerian scammer?' Louise said worriedly, making Anne-Marie bristle with indignation.

'No, I've seen his photo. He does exist,' Nina said, jumping in.

'Yeah, me too. He's pretty handsome, isn't he?' Louise sounded like she was swooning, and Anne-Marie felt pride in her clever choice of beau and instantly forgave Louise for her earlier insult.

'Yes, he is. And apparently, he has bags of money and a swanky lifestyle, so he's perfect for our Anne-Marie.'

Mmm, maybe a little harsh, Nina? What was she implying?

Moving back from the staircase, Anne-Marie decided to start again and crept back to her bedroom. Composing herself and fixing her smile once more, she opened and then loudly closed her bedroom door and stomped to the stairs.

'Hey, girls, what are you up to? Shall we get drinks on the go?' she called out breezily, walking down to the lounge room.

And so the act continued.

CHAPTER 15: MATTHEW
Tuesday 7 November

Matthew was the first to arrive in the makeshift Police HQ after a long night with Reynor both at the scene and drinking together in his hotel room until the early hours.

The tyre tracks were measured and photographed, and a second discarded butt had been found. They would be tested in Sydney.

He could see a phone message scribbled on a notepad on his desk from Constable Dillon, and he grimaced when he read it. He had been so caught up with investigating Madeline Bright's case that he hadn't updated the family of sixteen-year-old Ella Williams, who were naturally asking if it was their daughter who had been found.

Seeing that it was nearly seven thirty a.m., he decided to bite the bullet and picked up his phone. He hoped he was calling with good news, although after a year of not knowing, he couldn't be sure.

What would be worse? Remaining in an ongoing state of torturous limbo or having your worst fears confirmed?

Walking into the View café afterwards, Matthew ordered a bacon-and-egg roll and long black and walked over to the side to wait. It was only then that he noticed Louise. Her warm smile was just the antidote he needed after his wrenching twenty-minute conversation with an overwrought and highly emotional Ava Williams. Ella's mother had been anticipating his call, and Matthew was relieved to have at least beaten the news cycle in delivering the update to her.

'Hey, Matthew,' Louise said brightly, leaning in to peck his cheek. 'I'm glad to run into you as we are just about to head off. Just grabbing the mandatory coffees for the drive back.'

'Back to Canberra?'

'Yeah, and then the others will continue on to Sydney,' she answered before appearing to study him. 'How's it going here? You look weary.'

Clearly his late night with Reynor and the draining phone call he had just made were evident, but he tried for upbeat. 'Yeah, all good. We're getting there. I'll probably head back later today or tomorrow after we see what the day brings.'

After collecting a tray of coffees, Louise turned to give Matthew a hug.

'Don't be a stranger now? Let's meet up or come over for a meal one night,' she suggested, her dimples on full display.

Matthew promised to keep in touch, but would he? It had been twenty-five years since their last get-together, and as Louise walked away, the thought of not seeing her for another lifetime made him feel as bleak as he had moments earlier when he had hung up from Ava Williams. The momentary lift he had received from Louise's sparkling eyes and easy smile quickly disintegrated.

Watching Louise leave, he was determined to keep his word and make more room in his life for old friends. Decision made, he returned his focus to the bustling café and the bacon-and-egg roll with his name on it.

CHAPTER 16: NINA

Nina's skin was itching with impatience to get going on their drive back to Sydney. She had virtually gulped the mug of scalding green tea Louise had handed her ten minutes earlier when they had pulled up at Louise's home in Canberra.

'Thanks for the cuppa, Louise,' she said brightly, looking over to Anne-Marie with beseeching eyes and beginning to gather her jacket and handbag from the sofa.

'But what about your sandwich?' Louise enquired, looking confused. 'I'm starving and you girls must be too? Theodore's out in the kitchen making them now.'

'No, that's fine, love. I'm keen to get back before peak-hour traffic.' Nina was desperate to catch David in his office before closing time, but she wasn't about to broadcast that to her friends.

'Why don't we take them with us?' suggested Anne-Marie, clearly picking up on Nina's urgency to get going, and she hurried off in search of Theodore and their lunch.

'You okay, love?' Louise asked, looking at Nina with concern.

'Fine,' Nina said dismissively, before softening her reply. 'It's just that we've still got three hours driving ahead of us, so I don't want to get too relaxed and comfortable in your lovely home.' Her words did the trick, and Louise gave her a warm smile before offering to hurry up adorable Theodore who was out there making their gourmet feast. He really was the most doting husband, and Louise was lucky to have him.

Theodore wasn't who she would have imagined Louise marrying, but they were so right for each other. He was solid, dependable and nurturing, balancing her friend's creative, sometimes scatty, yet always endearing ways. When Louise had introduced the conservative, intellectual engineer to them twenty years ago, she and Nina had been surprised because he was so different to the grungy muso Rex, whom Louise had dated on and off forever. But the change agreed with her, and a year later Louise and Theodore had settled down to await the birth of their daughter Chloe.

Unfortunately, Theodore's attributes only served to remind Nina of David's deficiencies and what awaited her when she returned to Sydney. If only she could claim her husband was as dependable and solid. Had he ever been?

'Okay, here we go, straight from chef Theo's kitchen,' announced Anne-Marie, handing over a foil-wrapped sandwich. She was the only one who got away with abbreviating Theodore's name and exchanged a mischievous grin with him.

'Smoked leg ham, vintage cheddar and rocket with seeded mustard and cranberry sauce,' Anne-Marie announced, sniffing the package dreamily before giving Theodore a final hug.

Kissing Theodore and Louise goodbye, they walked to the car.

Nina clicked her remote, and automatically the roof of her electric blue MINI lifted and folded back into itself, switching her car into convertible mode. She was desperate for fresh air to clear her head and took enormous gulps of it as she steered them out of the Canberra suburbs. She listened half-heartedly to Anne-Marie's chatter, and eventually conversation ceased as Anne-Marie rested her seat back and closed her eyes.

The silence was blissful.

****

'Is he in?' Nina growled at David's executive assistant as she marched past her desk, yanking open David's office door before closing it firmly behind her.

'Nina!' David gasped, leaping to his feet. 'I thought I'd see you at home tonight?'

'Why haven't you called me back?' she barked.

'Oh, honey. I've been flat out,' he spluttered, not moving from his desk as if the protective barrier would save him from her wrath.

'I'm your bloody wife!' she yelled, furious now that she *finally* had his attention. 'I've been worried sick about my credit card. What's the deal?'

'Well, I... It's complicated,' he stammered, sitting back in his chair.

'Okay, so you know about the $22,000 charges. They're legit?' she asked, partially relieved because at least there would be an explanation.

He nodded mutely.

'And?'

'Let's talk about this tonight. I've got a client calling.' He refreshed his iPhone sitting silently on his desk to read the time.

'I've waited long enough, David. Tell me what this is all about.'

'I sort of had to move money about,' he mumbled, biting his lip worriedly.

'Sorry? Why?'

'My accounts were light on, and I needed a fast cash injection. But don't worry. It will all be returned pronto,' he said, producing a cavalier smile and starting to fuss around his desk as if the matter was concluded.

'Your business accounts or mine?' she asked, sitting down in front of him, now gritting her teeth.

'Ummm, mine,' he mumbled, not looking up but instead intently engrossed in shuffling papers.

'So, you maxed out my credit card for your business? What about your company bank accounts? Or your own bloody credit card?' Her anger surged once more.

He looked up at her raised voice and stopped what he was doing, sitting back in his chair.

'Darling, it's complicated. Just trust me,' he said in an effort to pacify her. And the reassuring tone gave her some semblance of comfort.

'I will explain everything tonight. But I really need to be on this call in about'—he refreshed the mute mobile once more—'about a minute. It's important, Nins. Believe me the business needs it. I'll then take you out for a delicious dinner tonight and explain it all,' he soothed, delivering another smile.

'Yes, but who's paying?' she snapped, standing up and storming out.

CHAPTER 17: ANNE-MARIE
Wednesday 8 November

Anne-Marie's face was bright red from the exertion of the Body Pump class she had just done, and her body felt heavy and lethargic from the forty-five-minute intense workout.

As she dragged off her sweaty black Lycra in the women's change room afterwards, she tuned into the noisy chatter around her from the bubbly twenty- and thirty-year-olds who had also done her class. Their energy and lithe shapes made her feel every day of her fifty years. Old and worn out.

A petite and naked woman to her left had an intricate butterfly tattoo on her hip and was slipping into sexy purple lingerie. Anne-Marie tried to recollect when she had last worn a lacy G-string. She had better get with the program as there were only two days before Henry arrived for their romantic tryst.

Making a mental note to visit the lingerie section of David Jones on her lunch hour, Anne-Marie wrapped a towel around her red splotchy body, grabbed her toiletries and limped towards the shower cubicles.

An hour later she was settled inside her glass office tower, scanning the plethora of emails in her inbox, her immaculately applied make-up, blow-dried shoulder-length hair and charcoal grey Theory pencil dress restoring her to her more poised appearance.

As a corporate travel consultant at Executive Traveller, she was the go-to girl for many of the big companies in town, overseeing their global travel arrangements with efficiency and results.

As she nibbled on her fruit toast, she put a red flag alongside the more urgent emails in her inbox. A total of eight mini crises would require her immediate attention this morning. One was a PWC senior executive who had been waylaid in Jakarta and needed her flights rearranged to Zurich and then Istanbul ASAP. Another was a group booking of thirty-two sales directors from Techforce who were due to fly out of Sydney on Monday for an internal gathering in Bali but now wanted to push back the get-together by two months and meet "somewhere in Queensland".

'What a nightmare,' she groaned quietly, annoyed at the hours she had already spent organising the Bali hotel rate as well as an adjacent conference room, a succession of restaurant bookings, transfers and assortment of cultural entertainment. 'Back to the starting point.' She decided to leave that one to last. It would take her hours.

Putting on her headset, she began to simultaneously dial numbers and send emails for the next three hours, hardly looking up except to nod for a takeaway coffee when one of the team offered to do a coffee run.

Eventually she wrenched off her headphones, pushed back her office chair and stood up to stretch. She could see that the floor was nearly empty now. Most of her twenty or so colleagues were out on their lunch break, and Anne-Marie reached for her handbag to go in search of food.

It was then that she noticed a text on her personal mobile phone from Henry.

Darling, two sleeps! xx

She smiled wickedly and sent back a dozen red love hearts before heading to the lift and the David Jones lingerie department, now finding an extra spring in her step.

CHAPTER 18: MATTHEW

The Sydney Homicide Squad had assumed control of the Mount Kosciusko case, and Matthew begrudgingly returned to his regular duties in the Queanbeyan police station.

Opening one file, only to close it and scan the next, he couldn't settle on any of the matters on his desk. His mind was consumed with Madeline Bright and how she came to be buried so far from home. He had asked to be kept in the loop, but he wasn't hopeful now that a Sydney team was running the investigation.

His mind shifted to Ella Williams, and he again began to puzzle over whether there was any connection to the missing sixteen-year-old snowboarder.

Reaching into the filing cabinet behind him, he extracted the paperwork on the case and began to read through the file notes once more. He hadn't looked at the folder for some months, and when he turned over the pages to her photograph, his breath caught in his throat.

Her pretty, innocent face smiled up at him, her brown eyes showing a hint of reproach at his failure to find her. The image had been shared extensively with police and locals at the time, and it was just one of many photos the family had on their phones, documenting the family ski trip sixteen months before.

A competent snowboarder, Ella had apparently insisted on "just one more run" of Thredbo Mountain before turning in for the day. Her parents had relented and taken their two youngest daughters back to the ski lodge. However, the Wollongong teenager never returned to the chalet. And she hadn't been sighted again.

The missing persons signs had been displayed throughout the village for six months or more, and regular pleas had been posted on both the Mountain Ski Resort Facebook page as well as the Kosciusko National Park social media channels for the best part of a year, but to no avail. Whilst comments of sympathy and support were aplenty, no concrete clues had been found.

Matthew recalled the enormous manhunt that had been assembled to search for Ella on the morning after her disappearance. A team of more than thirty police, National Parks & Wildlife volunteers and Thredbo's world-class ski patrol had gone out to look for her, despite the horrendous conditions. He had been among them.

Mother Nature, however, had turned against them. A huge dump of snow had arrived overnight, and by sunrise the howling winds were an intense one hundred kilometres an hour, creating blizzard conditions. It had been bitterly cold and, worse than that, not stable enough for aircraft, so the helicopters equipped with infra-red sensors couldn't take off to assist with precious eyes from the sky. When the wind had finally settled down late on day two of the search, the only evidence of humanity that the aircraft could see was the search team below, scrambling across the thick snow to find anything belonging to Ella.

For weeks the frantic routine had continued and had included police dog squads and seasoned backcountry skiers, but nothing had turned up. No traces of Ella Williams had been found.

Then the rumours that Ella had hitchhiked out of the resort began to surface, and with no evidence forthcoming from the hundreds of hours invested in the three-week search, the operation was scaled back and eventually abandoned. Police efforts were directed into other scenarios from running away to kidnapping.

In the months that followed, Matthew had explored every lead and digested every detail of the case, and he knew the file inside and out. At her family's request, he hadn't yet filed a report to the coroner, such was their hope that she might just turn up out of the blue.

Matthew would never close the file on Ella Williams. He believed her fate would be revealed by the mountain around him when it was good and ready.

Almost a year and a half on, it was still a mystery. Matthew had never bought into the rumours that Ella had deliberately disappeared following the anonymous report of her hitchhiking out of Cooma. The theory had never been substantiated, turning up blanks despite an extensive media campaign at the time. He believed she had got into trouble off piste, yet despite a comprehensive search, no evidence supporting his theory had been found either.

Matthew sat staring at the photo of Ella. She was dressed in brightly coloured ski gear, which he figured would have been hard to miss on the blanket of white snow if she had had an accident. A hot pink ski jacket with matching goggles, which sat on the rim of her black helmet. Long blond plaits hung halfway down her back.

He was lost in thought when his landline rang.

'Calucci! You're off to Sydney!' announced Rita, his boss's no-nonsense assistant.

'Sydney?'

'Commissioners approved an on-loan transfer to HQ. Sydney Homicide. Drowning in cases. Need assistance. Madeline Bright case. Said you offered?' Rita had an abrupt way of speaking. She dispensed with all but the most essential words in her haste to transfer messages. It was almost as if she were a talking telegram.

Hanging up not long after, given Rita's preference for scant information, Matthew pushed Ella's photo and the other documents back into the file.

He was about to return the folder to his filing cabinet, when he hesitated.

Time to hit the road, Ella, he thought, stashing the folder into his tattered brown leather briefcase. Let's see what we can find out.

CHAPTER 19: LOUISE
Thursday 9 November

'So what time is Romeo arriving?' Louise asked playfully, sitting down on a stool with her phone tucked under her ear, ready to hear about Anne-Marie's exciting weekend plans.

But she was met with silence at the other end. Louise looked down at her phone to check their connection and was about to repeat her question when Anne-Marie eventually replied.

'Sadly, something's come up.' Anne-Marie sounded indifferent. Not emotional. More… detached.

'Henry's not coming now?' Louise asked tentatively, determined not to overreact.

'He's just so busy with work.' Anne-Marie's voice was too calm. Almost sadly resigned.

'Oh love, you were so looking forward to finally meeting him.' Louise tried for a sympathetic tone, knowing how upset Anne-Marie would be and wishing she were looking at her face to read the signs. This was now the third time the mysterious Perth boyfriend had reneged on meeting face-to-face.

'It's fine, Lou. It's his work. There's some crisis that's just blown up, and he's the only one who can sort it.' Anne-Marie was already excusing him, which made

Louise bite back the criticism she was about to let fly. Instead, she rolled her eyes. It was perhaps fortunate that she was sitting three hundred kilometres away in her jewellery shop in Kingston; otherwise, she might have been tempted to shake some sense into her girlfriend.

Four months had passed since Anne-Marie had met the apparently fabulous Henry Dales through an online dating app, and yet she was still to meet him in person. Something seemed fishy to Louise, but whenever she raised her concerns, Anne-Marie went on the defensive.

'What about the Langham Hotel reservation? Your dinner at Tetsuya's?' Louise probed.

'It's fine, Louise,' Anne-Marie said breezily. 'I'll just reschedule our bookings.'

Louise sensed it wasn't that simple.

'Why don't you go to him!' Louise hadn't meant to blurt that out, but it made perfect sense, and they would finally get to meet properly.

'I offered,' Anne-Marie responded somewhat despondently. 'He's just so busy. It's fine. Really. We will just do it again in a few weeks or so. Anyway, how are you?' Anne-Marie clearly wanted to drop the subject.

Appreciating how hurt she must feel, Louise obliged and chatted about Theodore and how she missed never seeing Chloe, then the latest jewellery pieces she was working on, before Anne-Marie suddenly said she had to go.

Something was up with Anne-Marie, and it had a lot to do with Henry Dales, Louise thought. If Anne-Marie didn't want to delve, then perhaps she would.

For a smart woman, Anne-Marie had the blinkers on when it came to the smooth-talking Perth businessman.

She pressed Nina's number and, after getting her voicemail, asked her to call.

Together they would work out a plan to find out why Mr Dales was so elusive.

CHAPTER 20: NINA

Nina had seen Louise's name light up on her phone, but she couldn't speak with her right now.

She was already running late for her three-o'clock meeting with Sassy Swift, the aspirational fashion influencer she had been pursuing for months. If she kept her waiting any longer, she'd risk alienating the mini celebrity altogether and jeopardising any chance of signing her. And right now Talent Time needed her star power.

'Sorry to keep you,' Nina said cheerfully, entering the conference room and walking over to shake hands with Sassy Swift.

'No worries, yeah,' the young woman replied enthusiastically, holding out a slight quivering hand featuring exquisitely long, painted fingernails, dazzling in a sparkling silver shade with minuscule pearl drops at the tips.

Sassy wore thick but expertly applied make-up and a highly stylised outfit—white lace top over pink bralette, flared denim jeans and sky-high black sandals with platform heels. Her long golden hair revealed scatterings of vivid pink and blue streaks and was pulled into a deliberately messy bun at the top of her head.

'Can I pour you a green tea? Or something else? Coffee perhaps? The team know this is my go-to beverage, but I appreciate that it's not everyone's taste.' Nina gave a light laugh.

'Is it okay if I have a Coke?' Sassy asked nervously.

'Of course!' Nina jumped up to get a bottle from the small fridge.

'So Sassy, you've been incredibly busy,' Nina said, handing over the beverage and sliding a glass across to her.

'It's been mad, yeah,' Sassy responded before taking a gulp directly from the bottle.

Nina deliberately sat back in her chair, something she had once read as a technique to encourage someone to talk. It worked.

'I did this full-on Insta series with Mecca,' Sassy obligingly continued. 'And then I shot a six-part video campaign with Scanlan & Theodore last week. And we head to Tahiti on Tuesday for a Craylee campaign? You know the champagne brand, yeah? Too cool!'

Sassy sounded amazed at her newfound success, and Nina warmed to her infectious enthusiasm and sweet humility. Despite the highly manufactured image she cultivated online, Sassy came across as the girl next door. With the addition of a killer wardrobe and make-up of course.

Sassy continued to talk. 'I've also got my own content series and tutorials plus consulting, so yeah, all really full on right now.' She rolled her eyes adorably.

'Congratulations,' said Nina sincerely. 'That's actually why I wanted to meet. How would you like us to manage all that for you? And more?' Nina smiled reassuringly at her potential client, whose eyes lit up at the prospect.

Topping up her tea, Nina outlined the different ways that Talent Time could manage the highly sought-after star's commitments and expand her profile both here and overseas.

An hour later Nina was showing Sassy out, and before she had a chance to hold out her hand, she was enveloped in a hug.

'Thank you so much,' Sassy gushed, clutching on to Nina as if she were her rescuer. And perhaps she was in a way, because Nina knew only too well the huge wave Sassy still had left to ride.

Nina walked back to her office to prepare the contract and was surprised to see a huge bouquet of red roses on her desk.

Slipping over the small envelope, she pulled out the card from David.

Roses are red,
Violets are blue,
Nina you are truly special
I love you.

Breathing in the scent from the long-stem blooms, Nina sighed. She loved roses, and David had found her weak spot with the gift even if she hadn't quite forgiven him for the stress over her credit card debt.

He had murmured his apologies for not talking to her before transacting the large amount but had explained that it had all transpired so quickly. The initial funding he was relying on to purchase shares had been delayed, and he had needed to source instant cash to "tide things over".

'I didn't want to disturb you on your girls' weekend,' David had soothed, topping up her wineglass at the Italian trattoria they had dined at on Wednesday night.

'It's just a temporary loan. I promise, darling. Two, three days tops, and you will have your money back. Trust me,' he had said, squeezing her hand and lightly stroking her diamond ring. 'We are a team, darling.'

He had looked at her so adoringly, and his promises to repay the $22,000 had been repeated at least three times, and so Nina let the matter rest.

She needed to have faith in him. Surely he was only thinking of their future. Wasn't he?

CHAPTER 21: MATTHEW
Saturday 11 November

'Do you want to sit in on this one?' Detective Inspector Ian Devens asked Matthew, who had been poring over the expanding file of documents now related to the Madeline Bright case. It was Matthew's first day in the Surry Hills Police Headquarters, and he had been assigned a desk directly opposite Devens, the senior investigator on the homicide case.

There were two other junior detectives on the team, but both were out of the station at present. Matthew hadn't worked with any of them before, yet he was aware of Devens's slick reputation.

'Sure.' Matthew picked up his notepad and pen and stood up, eager to be hands-on.

'We've got Maddy's boyfriend, Jake Smith. It's our second interview. Let's see what we can extract.'

Matthew shrugged on his black jacket and followed Devens down the narrow hallway and into one of the many interview rooms that lined the corridor. Inside, a scruffy young man sat nervously picking at the gaping hole in the thigh of his jeans. His shaggy blond hair was held off his face by a pair of black Ray-Ban sunglasses, and his snug-fitting white T-shirt revealed a large swirling tattoo up the length of his muscular left arm.

He was good-looking but didn't advertise it with his ratty hair and light stubble.

Jake jumped to his feet when they walked in and nodded nervously. 'Hey,' he mumbled.

'Take a seat, Jake,' Devens said. 'I've got Detective Senior Sergeant Matthew Calucci with me.' He indicated Matthew, and all three men sat down at the conference table.

Detective Inspector Ian Devens was regarded as a supreme interviewer, and Matthew waited for him to take the lead, asking Jake to recount his last moments with his girlfriend on Friday 3 November.

'Like I said, I'm a tradie. A builder. We have to be on the tools at seven. I left the flat at just after six, say six-fifteen? I wanted to pick up a coffee on the way and get to the site before the owner left for the office. We needed his approval on a few things, so I had to catch him early.'

'Where was the project?' Devens asked, and Matthew listened as Jake expanded on the multimillion-dollar Seaforth home renovation project that had taken the best part of two years.

'And Madeline was at your flat on the morning on Friday 3 November?' Devens probed.

'Yeah. She was just getting up to hit the shower when I legged it to the truck.'

'How did she seem?'

'All good.' Jake shrugged, returning his gaze to his torn jeans.

'Was there anything out of the ordinary?'

Jake shook his head, biting his lower lip as if torn in sharing something more.

'Were you on good terms?'

He looked up abruptly. 'Yeah! Course.'

'You weren't fighting or anything?'

'No, everything was sweet,' he murmured.

'Then why didn't you notice she was missing all weekend?' Matthew asked, stepping into the interview.

Both men looked up at him sharply before Devens turned his stare to Jake. 'It's a good question, Jake?' He signalled they were waiting for an answer, crossing his arms.

'We didn't always hang out, you know?' Jake said defensively. 'She hung with her crowd, and I had footy and stuff on. We were both busy. I thought...' For the first time his easy-going demeanour cracked, and his eyes glistened with emotion, but he didn't continue his sentence.

'So, you didn't speak with her after Friday morning at your place?' Devens asked.

'No,' he said. 'But I tried. I texted her a few times and just figured she was going to get back to me when she was good and ready.'

'What do you mean "good and ready"?' Matthew queried, making a note to check Jake's mobile phone records.

'You know. When she could,' he mumbled.

Matthew was sure there was something Jake wasn't saying, and it had a lot to do with their last morning together. But he wouldn't push it. After all, Devens was now moving the interview along to details of Jake's movements over the forty-eight hours since he left the house.

'I was on the tools all day and got home just after four on Friday afternoon after a beer with the boys. I went to the gym for a few hours.'

'Then what did you do?' Devens asked.

'Just hung out at home. Got some takeaway delivered. Went to bed.'

'Were you alone?'

'Yeah. No. My flatmate, Moses, came in, and we watched NBL for a while and crashed out. Then I had footy practice and a game on Saturday and spent the night wasted with the boys at Stellars in Manly,' he said.

Matthew noted down Jake's movements, which unfortunately left very few windows of opportunity for Jake to slip away to Mount Kosciusko and back, a good twelve-hour return trip by car.

But that didn't put him entirely in the clear. There was something amiss, and he intended to find out what.

CHAPTER 22: ANNE-MARIE
Sunday 12 November

Anne-Marie stretched out in the luxuriously oversized bed and cast her eyes around the ornate suite of muted silvers, creams and beige. Despite what she had told Louise, she hadn't cancelled her booking at the Langham Hotel. It was non-refundable, which she wasn't going to admit because it would make her sound even more pitiful. Plus she didn't want Louise to think badly of Henry. Or perhaps *worse* was more apt. And that would be a hard task given Henry's no-show.

But he had been so apologetic and so, so thoughtful in sending those long-stemmed red roses. And their naughty photo session last night had been too much fun. For now, that would be enough.

Kicking off the soft cotton sheets, she padded past the empty champagne bottle and chocolate wrappers and into the enormous marble bathroom. Turning on the rain showerhead, she was instantly immersed in a blissful stream of warm water. Reaching for the L'Occitane shampoo, she began to hum happily, surrounded by so much delicious decadence.

She would check out after breakfast and return to the *real world*, her tiny Double Bay apartment, which would practically fit inside this beautiful hotel suite. It was a ridiculously tiny place to live, but rent was expensive in Sydney, and she wasn't going to buy into the property market on her own. No matter how much both Nina and Louise lectured her about it. What equity would she put into it? She lived hand to mouth these days, spending her wage on luxuries like this, and she didn't want to give that up. Soon enough she would be living with Henry in his palatial house anyway, so what was the point?

CHAPTER 23: MATTHEW

'I think we should talk to Jake's flatmate,' Matthew said by way of greeting when Devens arrived on Sunday morning.

Matthew pushed Moses Galvin's original statement across his desk and on to Devens before lifting his coffee mug—the third for the day, and it was only ten.

Matthew continued. 'He left the flat *after* Jake that morning. He's the last known person to have had any contact with Maddy.'

Devens looked at the document and then at Matthew. 'Yes, that's true, however, Moses said he didn't see Madeline at all on Friday morning?'

'Perhaps he heard something. A fight between Maddy and Jake earlier that morning or even the night before. Or a phone call or a car pulling up at the flat.'

'All right. Get him in. I've got a few more questions about his timeline anyway.'

'Why don't we call over there,' Matthew suggested. 'It would give me a chance to look over the flat. We might also get a feel for the dynamic. After all, they are both alibiing each other for Friday night.'

A couple of hours later, Matthew stood behind Devens as the inspector buzzed the doorbell to Jake and Moses's ground-floor apartment. It was a nondescript block of bland low-rise residential buildings that sprinkled the peninsular of the northern beaches of Sydney. Not close enough to offer ocean views but walkable to the beach, which would be the obvious appeal for surfies. The flight of stairs to the apartments above revealed threadbare carpet, and the marked walls could do with a fresh coat of paint, but Matthew guessed most tenants were renters and the landlords who owned these apartments wouldn't be racing to plough more money into their investments.

'Hey man,' said Moses, opening the door and leading them into a small dark lounge room. Matthew could see traces of last night's excesses in the galley kitchen as he walked past—a sea of empty beer bottles and pizza boxes littering the benchtop.

The lounge room looked conspicuously tidy, as if it had been hurriedly cleaned up in preparation for their visit and the debris hastily relocated to another room, the kitchen.

After completing the introductions, Devens enquired about Jake's whereabouts.

'Nah. He's at his folks in Nowra. He went down yesterday arvo.'

'Right. Well, we won't keep you long, Moses. We just need to ask a few more questions,' Devens said easily as Matthew studied him. Moses had a clean-shaven head and a light stubble on his chin, and his eyes looked less of their natural brown and more blearily bloodshot. He had the same rangy, muscly build as Jake but was significantly taller. Basketballer height.

'We want to piece together Madeline's final movements, and that brought us back to this flat,' Devens began. 'Can you tell us anything that you may have left out of your earlier statement? About the morning of Friday 3 November or even the night before? Did you notice anything? Hear anything?'

'Nah. Nothing. I've already said it all. I was hungover and didn't even get up until the afternoon. I surfed and stuff. Then just had a quiet one with Jake that night. That's it. Wish I could remember, hey.'

'What about work on Friday?' Matthew probed, recalling that Moses was a plumber.

'Nah. I called in sick. Slack, hey.' He exchanged a lopsided grin as if they were all in solidarity on that point.

Interesting work ethic, Matthew thought.

'How did Jake and Maddy seem?' Matthew asked.

'What do you mean?'

'Just generally? Did they look happy? Any arguments? Anything unusual happen on Thursday night or Friday morning? Or even before that?'

'Nah. All good with them. Yeah, sure she wanted him to commit. You know, get a place together. But he wasn't into it.'

'Madeline wanted Jake to move out and share a place together?' Devens asked.

'Yeah. But hey, all girls get like that, right?' He looked at them with a raised eyebrow and smirked quietly.

'What would that have meant for you?' asked Matthew, studying his face.

'No worries, hey. I'd just get another mate in to split the rent. No sweat. But Jake wasn't ready, you know.'

Jake and Moses had gone to school together since they were five, according to the file, and somehow Matthew didn't think Moses would be overjoyed to see his best mate coupled up at the age of thirty. These boys still seemed to be living a young man's lifestyle with their surfing, boozing and haphazard housekeeping.

'Just getting back to the night before Madeline disappeared. Did you recall hearing anything? Small, big, anything inside or even outside the apartment?'

'Nah. It's like I already said. I was out late, crashed when I came in and was hungover for half of Friday. Didn't hear a thing, mate,' he said, trying for a reassuring smile.

Matthew wasn't buying it.

CHAPTER 24: NINA
Monday 13 November

Nina and her senior account manager, Lee Lamone, were waiting in the agency's conference room for Sassy Swift, their new social media influencer, to arrive to officially sign on with them.

Nina would oversee the contractual side of things, as she did with all Talent Time's clients who were predominantly digital influencers like Sassy, as well as actors, models and artists. Lee would manage Sassy's public profile, and this morning Lee would run through the comprehensive PR schedule that had been drawn up for the next six months. Nina also wanted to broach a couple of potential brand partnerships, which would be a good fit for Sassy and prove lucrative too.

Because Sassy was flying out to Tahiti tomorrow for the Craylee Sparkling Wine campaign, Nina wanted everything signed off today. Especially because she was keen to announce the starlet's signing on Talent Time's own social channels.

It was now eleven-fifteen a.m. and Sassy was fifteen minutes late. Not unusual in the world of mini celebrities, but it had Nina fidgeting.

But then the door opened, and in sailed Sassy in an oversize red jumpsuit and stunning white Prada sneaker heels. Her hair was up in a high ponytail, and the vivid combination just screamed *fun*.

God, I wish I could have some of that, Nina mused, getting up to welcome their newest client.

The meeting went well, and after finalising everything, the conversation moved to Sassy's Tahiti trip the following day.

'Why don't you join me?' Sassy asked, a huge smile lighting up her already striking face.

'But isn't it tomorrow?' Nina said, flummoxed.

'Yeah,' she gushed enthusiastically. 'But my plus one fell through, and they've hired a private plane, so why not! You could be my guest. See what I do, yeah?'

Nina sensed Lee watching her, ready to pounce on the invitation which Nina would surely decline. And Nina almost obliged. But then she did the most uncharacteristic thing she had probably ever done in her professional career to date.

'I'd love to.' Nina's face lit up with excitement, something she hadn't felt for some time.

Lee looked startled, possibly never having seen Nina shrug off her busy work schedule before for a spontaneous island escape with a client.

'Great!' Sassy cheered, putting her hand up to high five Nina, who obliged, raising up her palm in joy.

Now over her shock, Lee gave Nina an admiring look as if to say, 'Go Nina!'

Who am I, and what have I done with the real me? Nina wondered.

CHAPTER 25: LOUISE

Louise arrived at her Kingston shop on Monday morning and unloaded her bags before flicking on the lights, air-conditioning and music. Just before turning over the OPEN sign, she glanced around the floor to check that everything was in its place.

A familiar buzz warmed her, and she grinned at what she had created—a bespoke jewellery atelier. Her one-stop shop for jewellery lovers stocked not only her own designs but the works of many other Australian jewellers, spanning contemporary to art deco and everything in between. Gemstones, crystals, silver and gold—everything was available and carefully displayed to create distinct sections enticing fans of colourful stones in one direction and pearl lovers in another.

'Morning Louise,' announced Mike, the postie, on opening the front door and handing over her mail.

'Good morning,' she responded, taking the uninteresting-looking bundle of letters and flyers.

'I hear your neighbour left,' he remarked, angling his head to the shop next door. Mike had been the local postman for decades and was always the first with the village gossip and was not shy in sharing it.

'Emma's Fashions?' she said. The dress shop had been unusually quiet of late and was closed last

Saturday, which was odd because that was the busiest day in retail. Louise had assumed the weekend closure was a one-off.

'Yeah, gone into receivership apparently, so the shopfront will be emptied out later this week,' he said knowingly, as if he had witnessed this scene many times before. As the resident postie of long standing, he probably had.

'Gosh, I feel awful for them. I never really got to know Emma, sadly.' Louise frowned, trying to recall the last time she had had a conversation with the young woman. 'She wasn't often in the shop, was she? I seemed to always see an array of different people in there, certainly over the past year anyway.'

'Yeah, I noticed that too. Anyway, maybe that's where it all went wrong,' he said, mulling that over. 'Anyway, I'd best get on. Have a great day, Louise.' He left her in the same chirpy mood he had arrived.

With no early-morning customers, Louise found herself in deep thought about the poor proprietor Emma and the soon-to-be-empty shop next door. Running a small business was hard work, and she felt a rush of sympathy for the woman who she had seen dashing in and out of the boutique only a few times over the past couple of years. But in all honesty, she couldn't recall when she had last seen her physically working there. Had it been months? This year at all?

Louise was relieved that her financial accounts were in good order. She was never going to take over the world with New Age Jewels, but she was earning more than enough to pay her overheads, contribute to the family accounts and put some aside for holidays and small luxuries.

Suddenly the empty space next door seemed less depressing as a thought sparked. Could she expand? Having the space would enable her to host jewellery classes with local artists, jewellers and silversmiths. This was something Louise had dreamed of doing for so long, but her own shop was too small to host such sessions.

Her mind swirled with a myriad of questions. How many people could she host in a workshop? How often would she run them? Would it be feasible? What would the rent cost?

Most of all, she thought this could be a real chance of spending more time with Chloe. Since her daughter had finished school last year and moved out, Louise hardly saw her and missed her terribly. She recalled the times, years before, when Chloe was just a child and they had sat together, making beaded necklaces, before progressing to wire and silver when she was in high school. Louise patiently instructing her young daughter and together realising the fruits of their creative endeavours. Chloe was incredibly creative, and Louise wondered if she appreciated what a talent she had.

Slipping back behind the shop counter, Louise began to jot down her thoughts on a notepad. After scribbling a rough concept, she would develop a viable business plan to review with Theodore tonight.

Louise was energised at the prospect of shaking things up, both with her business and her flailing relationship with her daughter.

CHAPTER 26: MATTHEW

'Okay, let's go through what we know. Madeline and Jake were planning to move out together.' Devens addressed Matthew, Sorenson and Davies around the communal meeting table late on Monday morning.

'I've just spoken again with Lizzie Riggs, Madeline's flatmate, and she has confirmed that Madeline and Jake were planning to get their own place early next year. It was well known within her shared house that she would be moving out in the new year to live with her boyfriend.'

'I wonder how Moses felt about that?' Matthew pondered aloud.

'Maybe pissed off, but that's all, surely,' said Davies, the youngest on the team. He had not long got out of uniform and was looking to the other plain clothes for their thoughts.

'Interestingly, Moses was a factor in Madeline's decision, according to Lizzie. She didn't feel comfortable in the flat with Moses, said he was *creepy*.'

'Creepy? In what way?' asked Sorenson, the only female on their team.

'Lizzie said he was always trying it on with suggestive comments, acting sleazy, that sort of thing,' Devens elaborated. 'Lizzie said she also felt the same way with Moses. I gather he's quite a lad and tries it on a lot.'

'Do you think that's all he was doing though?' Sorenson asked, frowning.

Matthew also wondered the same thing. If so, Moses had more to lose than just his flatmate moving out. He would lose access to Maddy and possibly her female household as well. Possibly even his mate if Maddy objected strongly enough to his antics.

'There's something bugging me about Moses. His casual attitude to this whole thing, plus his dismissive almost derogatory attitude to work, women… I don't know… I'd like to delve further,' Matthew announced to the team.

'Yes, sure. Look into past history, that sort of thing. See if anything pops up on the database too. Sorenson, I'd like you to talk to the other flatmates and see what else they might know about Jake and Moses. Any issues with Jake or whether Moses was overfriendly with them as well. That type of thing.'

Nodding, Sorenson wrote down a few things in her notebook.

'Nothing back yet on the DNA on the cigarette butts, and there won't be for a while. But the good news is the tyre impression gives us more information on make and type of vehicle, and I'll get you Davies to check that out,' he said, sliding over the email printout.

After a few more updates, they disbanded and returned to their desks. Matthew decided to follow the work lead first and looked up the phone number for WeWork Plumbing.

The receptionist confirmed that Moses had phoned in sick on Friday 3 November, just after eight o'clock.

Interesting, thought Matthew, for someone who slept "half the day" hungover.

His employment file revealed he had been with the firm for just on six months and had taken a total of nine sick days and four more "leave without pay" days since he had started there.

Prior to that, Moses had worked in a range of other plumbing jobs. Many short term and none longer than a year. Looking at the list of companies, Matthew began to search for their phone numbers and dial.

An hour later, he had a short three-year work history for Moses, which included five plumbing firms and then periods of a few months when he didn't appear to work at all. July to September every year. Interesting. I wonder why? thought Matthew.

CHAPTER 27: ANNE-MARIE
Tuesday 14 November

Anne-Marie had been drowning in airline schedules for the past two days and had finally come up for air. Booking flights for clients, changing itineraries and rerouting travel plans for others. She knew how to secure the best fares as well as negotiate upgrades and was a master at avoiding cancellation fees, leveraging Frequent Flyer points and finding the best seats for her clients. Anne-Marie considered herself something of an expert when it came to knowing how the airlines worked and navigating around the complex travel booking system in front of her.

What if she snuck in her own flight booking? she wondered. *A flight to Perth, for example.*

The idea gave her delicious goose bumps. Imagine Henry's expression on seeing her arrive in his hometown! Would she surprise him at his office? March in like she had an important meeting with Mr Henry Dales. Ha ha. No, that would probably put him in an awkward position, or he might not be available which would ruin the moment of surprise. What about if she waited outside his office and casually walked up to him instead? Maybe she could pretend to be lost and ask him for directions and then see how long it took him to twig that it was her.

Anne-Marie imagined the enormous grin on his sexy face and his eyes devouring her in the flesh when he realised it was actually her. That's not all she would like devoured, she thought naughtily, releasing a loud giggle.

Looking around the quiet office, she was relieved no one had looked up. She refreshed her computer screen and pulled up her Qantas account.

It was time to woo Henry. After all, if the mountain won't come to Muhammad, then Muhammad must go to the mountain… and all that.

Her crossed legs jiggled under her desk as she excitedly tapped in dates and awaited the flight schedule to load.

CHAPTER 28: NINA
Wednesday 15 November

Tahiti was as glorious as Nina had envisaged. The clear, crystal waters and white, white beaches were as divine as the tourism hype.

Since arriving two days ago, Nina had been instantly transformed by the beauty and calm. Strolling along the sandy shoreline in her newly acquired floral sarong and enormous straw hat, Nina marvelled at her good fortune in being here. It was so unlike her to be spontaneous, but when Sassy Swift had invited her to join her on the Craylee shoot, she had been compelled to accept. Perhaps there was an unconscious urge to run away from David for a while. Nina was still annoyed at his sneakiness in using her credit card without asking but knew that she needed to get over it and move on. Being here was the perfect way to put distance between it and him. It also provided a window seat to watch her new acquisition in action. Social media influencers had magnetic appeal, amassing enormous followings, and whilst Nina was across Sassy's prolific feeds on Instagram and Facebook, it was rare to witness how the magic happened.

Sassy was in hair and make-up at the hotel and would be for the next hour and a half, giving Nina this window of time to enjoy a meditative walk along the long stretch of beach before she went back to watch the shoot.

A pop-up party scene had been set up at one end of the beach, and in a few hours' time it would be buzzing with actors and bit players creating a stylish soirée on the envious location. The set included an enormous timber deck, whitewashed lounge chairs and yellow Craylee umbrellas. Large silver buckets that would soon be filled with ice and crates of the sparkling wine. She had been invited to join the party scene as an extra but preferred to stand back and watch. Plus she wanted to take photographs for her own company's Instagram page, which would be uploaded when the campaign was officially launched.

It was a rookie mistake to let the cat out of the bag on a big brand campaign like this, and Nina had thankfully never fallen for it. Although she hadn't hesitated to announce the agency's signing of Sassy Swift the afternoon before she left. It had been heart-warming to read the many messages of congratulations from clients and industry colleagues.

'Enjoying the sunshine?'

Nina looked up from her thoughts to see Dermott Sage, the Craylee wine executive she had met the night before at the welcome drinks at the hotel. He must have been walking towards her from the opposite end of the beach; she vaguely recalled seeing a figure in the distance before her mind had wandered off.

'It's stunning.' She smiled, looking out to sea.

'Yes, isn't it?' He followed her gaze, and they stood peacefully for a few moments, watching the waves lightly rise before breaking and rolling into shore.

'I thought you would be setting up the shoot?' Nina turned to look at Dermott, who was dressed casually in a white T-shirt and blue floral board shorts and a Craylee cap. He was about the same age as Nina, but he could pass for ten years younger in his beach attire. A light tan added to his youthful look.

'The advertising agency seems to have it all under control, so I thought I'd go AWOL for half an hour or so and then head back. Can I walk with you?'

They wandered on along the sand, Dermott expanding on how he came to be working for the South Australian-based wine company.

'I didn't know too much about wine when I joined Craylee three years ago, well apart from what I liked,' he said with a light laugh. 'My specialty is really building brands, and it's been pleasing to see the brand recognition we've achieved over the past few years for Craylee.'

He was being modest, Nina thought, given the huge name the sparkling wine label now commanded. It was the beverage associated with glamorous events and celebratory occasions from Melbourne Cup's glamorous Bird Cage fixtures to the prestigious Tag Heuer "round the world yacht" challenge.

'So why Sassy? She seems younger than your normal demographic?'

'Yeah, that was deliberate. We want to get to the younger market—the twenty- to thirty-year-olds who we haven't traditionally tapped into before. We're launching a new range, Craylee +, and Sassy is just perfect for it.' He paused, looking at his watch. 'Anyway, I should be heading back. Will I see you there?' he asked hopefully.

'Yes, I'll definitely be watching.'

'Are you sure I can't convince you to be on the deck?' he asked teasingly.

'I think I'm outside the demographic.' Nina shooed away the invitation to be part of the party scene.

'Not at all. You would add a serious touch of sophistication,' he said kindly, before breaking into a light jog in the direction they had just walked.

****

By the time Nina had showered and arrived at the shoot, it was in full swing. There must have been one hundred or more people on the set—a combination of actors, extras and musicians as well as the dozen Sydney advertising guys behind it all.

The vibe was electric, and at the centre of it all was Sassy, looking stunning in a gold lamé dress with her glossy mane of now strawberry blonde hair hanging femininely over her shoulders and down her back. The pastel tips had vanished, and her overall look reeked of true glamour.

'Nina, you're here!' Sassy came bouncing over to hug her.

'You look gorgeous.' Nina stood back to admire her.

'Yeah? It's cool, yeah?' Sassy beamed with pleasure and did a quick twirl. In moments she was recalled to the set.

'She's quite a find,' Dermott said, joining Nina on the side of the deck and handing her a small bottle of chilled mineral water with a paper straw.

He had changed into cargo shorts and a floating white linen shirt and looked like he should be in the campaign himself.

Accepting the drink gratefully, they fell back into easy conversation with Dermott occasionally slipping away to adjust the angle of a Craylee wine bottle or provide approval of a particular camera angle.

It gave Nina time to observe Sassy and her easy way with the camera. She was a natural all right.

Nina felt utterly happy and attempted to capture the moment by snapping off a dozen photos of Sassy, the stunning beach behind her and even a fun selfie, just for her.

CHAPTER 29: LOUISE

Louise had just presented her business plan, and the boisterous applause generated a giggle. But her audience was hardly objective.

'It's splendid! Bravo,' cheered an adoring Theodore from the sofa.

'Do you think it sounds okay?' She was anxious to get this right.

'Of course! You've put so much detail into everything, from how the new shop will be refurbished—and very economically too I might add—to how you would utilise the space to boost profits for New Age Jewels. My love, you've done more than you needed to. Go get 'em,' he said, planting a kiss on her lips.

Louise had spent hours and hours crunching the numbers. She had carefully worked out what she could afford in her budget to lease the new property and done some rough projections on the income the new studio would generate from adult and children's classes as well as exclusive masterclasses. She had also drawn up a potential calendar of events and exhibitions for the next twelve months. According to her projections, New Age Jewels would reflect a tidy profit within the first year of operation.

'You've always been my number one supporter.' Louise squeezed Theodore's hand. 'Thank you.'

He gathered her into his arms, and it was the best feeling in the world. Theodore's warm body felt like home.

Her husband's effusiveness for the expansion had prompted Louise to telephone Chloe to share her exciting news, but she had only got to leave a message. Chloe rarely, if ever, answered her mobile, and Louise should know by now just to text. But she had really wanted to talk with her, have an actual conversation instead of short, intermittent texts. Hopefully Chloe would be in touch soon so they could catch up properly. She was worried about her.

Since moving out of home at the start of the year, Chloe had been hard to pin down. Louise knew she had to loosen the apron strings, but she missed hanging out with her daughter. Chloe was embracing a gap year, and that entailed moving out of home and quite a lot of partying it seemed.

'It would be so uncool to live at home,' she had nagged until her parents had eventually relented. They were paying her rent on a share house, which was more than they had expected, but Theodore had highlighted that the Canberra rental market was the most expensive in the country and so it was to be expected.

'We don't want her slumming it in a dive with half a dozen flatmates,' he had warned.

Too right, she thought, although later recalled doing exactly that when she was an eighteen-year-old fresh out of school.

Chloe lived with two friends, Emily and Ben, in a suburb on the other side of Canberra, closer to the university scene.

'If I had a car, I could visit more,' Chloe had said one day when Louise had protested about never seeing her. Perhaps they would splash out and buy her one for her nineteenth birthday. Or would that be too extravagant?

But even with a car, Louise wasn't sure that Chloe would become a frequent visitor. She had become consumed by her new freedom. Chloe had a part-time bar job a few nights a week at a club that finished in the early hours of the morning and often resulted in her sleeping through half the day. She was also experimenting with making clothes, which she sometimes sold at the weekend markets around Canberra and the ACT.

Yes, Chloe had a lot on, and Louise just had to accept that her daughter didn't have time to hang out with the old ones at home. That would definitely be "uncool".

CHAPTER 30: MATTHEW

'Okay, troops, let's gather around,' said Devens, striding in with a file in one hand and a coffee in the other.

'The autopsy reveals Madeline was strangled, the ligature marks around her neck and haemorrhaging in the eyes are obvious signs, and the report confirms it. Hands were the weapon, so we're narrowing that to a male based on the size and force. The forensic evidence indicates the strangulation occurred elsewhere and she was later buried in the snow.'

He regarded them solemnly before taking a seat. 'So, what have we got? Hit me with it.' Devens looked expectantly at them all, before Davies jumped in.

'Yeah, we've narrowed the vehicle type to a list of five all midsize pickup trucks or SUVs. The boyfriend has one that would fit, but then again so do most tradies in Sydney.'

'Most tradies in Sydney don't have a connection though, do they?' Devens said, raising an eyebrow at him.

'What about the flatmate's vehicle? What does Moses drive?' asked Matthew.

'Yeah, like I said, all the tradies seem to fit the same three or four models. They have the same make, slightly different model Toyota Hilux ute. Jake's is a 2016 model and Moses's is a 2019.'

'Pretty chummy,' Sorenson remarked, 'driving around in twin utes.'

Turning his attention to Sorenson, Devens looked torn between glaring at her or taking on board her observation. 'What did you learn about young Moses from Madeline's flatmates?' Devens asked instead.

Sorenson proceeded to share the feedback from Maddy's three female flatmates.

'Basically, they all say that Moses is a definite sleaze. Doesn't know when to back off, and they wouldn't want to be left alone with him,' she summed up.

'Sounds like a charmer,' Davies scoffed.

'But apparently there's a guy at Maddy's school that they said has been pestering her as well. Another teacher,' Sorenson added. 'I've arranged an appointment with the principal of Blue Leaf Public later today and can find out if any complaints were lodged.'

'Also speak with the teacher involved,' Devens said. 'Who is it?'

'Clayton Jones. He apparently teaches the grade five and six students.'

'Matthew, go with Sorenson and see what this Clayton Jones has to say for himself,' Devens ordered before dismissing them all.

****

At two that afternoon, Matthew and Lisa Sorenson sat waiting outside the Blue Leaf Primary School principal's office, and it gave Matthew a momentary smirk. In all his school years, he had never been told to "go to the principal's office", and yet now at the ripe old age of forty-nine, he was doing just that.

Sorenson had been in uniform for six years before transitioning to plain clothes, and this was her first significant case. Her first homicide. She had excellent people skills and a solid work ethic, which Matthew admired in such a young detective.

'Mr George is ready to see you now,' said the matronly assistant, leading them into the headmaster's office.

'Sorry to keep you,' Mr George said, fussing to show them into the room before indicating the seats for them to take.

'Now how can I be of assistance? I believe this is in relation to poor Madeline Bright. We are all so upset by the news.' His small round eyes darted about behind his wire-framed glasses.

'Please know that we are doing everything we can to solve this matter,' said Sorenson.

'We understand that you have a fellow teacher here, a Clayton Jones. What can you tell us about Clayton Jones?' Matthew asked.

'Oh?' The principal looked perplexed. 'Do you think he had something to do with Madeline's death?'

'At this stage we are just gathering a wide range of information,' Sorenson soothed.

'Oh. Okay then. Well, Clayton has been a teacher here for two years now. He instructs the senior students—grades five and six.'

When neither of them commented, the principal quickly realised that they were awaiting more insights.

'Ummm. What else can I tell you? Clayton seems to be well suited to teaching and is popular with the students and... other teachers, I believe.' He didn't look convinced.

'How have you found Clayton on a personal level?' Sorenson asked.

'Oh... ummm. Well, as I said, he seems to be a solid type. Ummm...' Mr George laughed awkwardly. 'You see we have nearly thirty teachers here, so I must admit to not having a thorough knowledge of their personal lives—that type of thing.'

'Have there been any issues with Clayton Jones during his time at the school?' Matthew asked.

'No. Well, not really.'

'What do you mean not really?' Matthew asked.

'Oh, there was something brought to my attention just before the July school holidays, but it was all sorted.'

Matthew was finding the evasive Mr George tiresome, and his reluctance to just get things out on the table was grating.

'Perhaps we could inspect his employment file?' Sorenson asked in a bright, upbeat voice.

'Oh. Well, I'm not sure that's possible. It's sensitive private data you see.'

'Mr George. This is a murder investigation. We have a witness informing us that this man may be of interest to our investigation, and we therefore expect your full cooperation,' Matthew said firmly, and the effect was instant. Mr George jumped up as if he had been scalded and hurried over to retrieve a manila folder from one of the grey filing cabinets on the other side of the room, bringing it back to his desk.

He opened it up and flicked through a few pages before pulling out the relevant document, handing it over to the detectives.

Scanning it now, Matthew could see there had been two complaints lodged in the past year in relation to sexual harassment. One complaint was made by a fellow teacher in March, and the other was by a parent and teacher committee member, following a P&C fundraising event in July. There was no reference to Madeline Bright.

'Were these matters investigated by police?' Matthew asked, already knowing the answer.

Mr George looked sheepish before defending the school's own internal investigation processes.

'Mrs Beverley Taellow withdrew the complaint afterwards,' he said, referring to the P&C member. 'There had been some alcohol consumed, and their accounts varied quite dramatically, so it was agreed that we would just leave it at that.'

'And the teacher—Miss Katie Allowster?' Sorenson asked, referring to the earlier complaint.

'Katie was just a supply teacher for one term, and she had another school lined up after the Easter break. Again, the matter was investigated thoroughly, and we had a word to Clayton Jones about behaviour at social functions put on by the school... and with female members of the school community.'

'Were there other incidents?' Matthew probed. 'No, no, no.' Mr George shook his head vigorously.

'What was the relationship like between Clayton Jones and Madeline Bright?' Matthew asked.

'Fine. As far as I know,' the principal said, shrugging his shoulders. Matthew wasn't overly confident that Mr George would be in the know on such matters and requested the contact details for the two female complainants so that they could speak to them and better understand what happened in each case.

'And we would also like to now speak with Clayton Jones,' Matthew said. 'Where can we find him?'

Mr George looked like he was about to decline, but the stern look on Matthew's face and the soft, encouraging smile from Sorenson had him picking up his phone.

'Julie, would you please have Clayton Jones join us?'

CHAPTER 31: ANNE-MARIE

Anne-Marie's plan to surprise Henry would need to be put on ice. No sooner had she booked her flights for the upcoming weekend, when she received a late-night photo of him blowing her a kiss outside the Perth airport, bound for Dubai.

Gorgeous, miss you already. Urgent business xx

How long will you be there? Anne-Marie quickly texted back.

1 week? xx His text pinged.

When can we talk? she typed and then anxiously waited for his response.

Soon my darling xx

WTF? Tossing her phone onto the coffee table, she let out a groan. *What am I doing?*

She walked to the fridge and yanked it open and plucked out a bottle of Riesling and unscrewed the cap. Sloshing a hefty amount into a wineglass, she found some brie and crackers and sat back at the sofa with her late-night snack. She flicked the remote, searching for something distracting to watch and landed on *Killing Eve*. More like *Killing Henry* she thought, and pressed Play.

About half an hour later her phone buzzed, and she snatched it up from the table, but it was a group message to her and Nina from Louise.

Sweeties, I'm coming to Sydney! Dinner at Picolo? Saturday 8pm? Lou xx

At least her weekend had been salvaged, Anne-Marie thought, texting back a heart emoji before switching her attention back to maniacal Eve on her screen.

Little did she realise what Lou had in store.

CHAPTER 32: MATTHEW

Clayton Jones was thin and pale with a small moustache that seemed at odds with his baby face. Perhaps he was trying to look older than he was, more consequential, Matthew pondered.

The skinny, awkward man in front of them didn't quite fit the image Matthew had conjured up, but two internal complaints plus Maddy's comments to her flatmates were compelling.

Clayton looked like a startled rabbit when he arrived at the principal's office. Matthew requested a private meeting room or empty classroom so that he and Sorenson could speak with the teacher, and Mr George willingly offered up his office, almost running for the door in relief to be excused from further questions.

'Would you tell us about your dealings with Madeline Bright?' Matthew asked, observing the beads of sweat forming across Clayton's forehead as he settled into his chair.

'We were colleagues,' he squeaked, his upward inflection giving the impression he wasn't entirely sure if he had answered correctly.

'Was there more to your relationship than that?' Sorenson probed, giving a small nod to encourage the man to share more. And it did the trick.

'Well, yes… We were friends. I really liked Madeline and just can't believe the terrible news.' His eyes glistened, and he wiped them with the back of his hands.

'Did you hang out together? That type of thing.' Sorenson continued, allowing Matthew to sit back and observe Clayton's body language and any telltale signs that he wasn't answering truthfully. Touching his face, playing with his hair and not blinking were obvious ones; however, Clayton didn't do any of those. Instead, his Adam's apple bobbed furiously as he nervously talked about his friendship with Maddy, recounting sharing his homebaked frittata with her one day and sometimes joining her on a lunchtime stroll if neither of them was on playground duty.

'Were you interested in a romantic relationship with Maddy?' Sorenson asked gently.

'No!' Clayton shook his head vehemently from side to side. 'She had a b-b-boyfriend.'

He put on a convincing image, but there was obviously more to the stumbling, good Samaritan based on the formal complaints that had been lodged.

Taking over the interview, Matthew increased the tempo.

'When did you last see Maddy?'

'On Thursday. She didn't come to school on Friday.'

'Okay, so you didn't see her at all on Friday. Can you account for your own movements on Friday?'

'Yes, of course. I was here first thing to supervise the play rehearsal for the senior students. We are putting on a production of *Alice in Wonderland*. I was here at seven thirty to meet the students in the play at the school hall so we could get an hour of rehearsal in before school started. I taught for the rest of the day.' His voice was calm and betrayed no hint of fear.

'What did you do after school finished?' Matthew asked.

'We had a run-through of the second part of the play after school, and I went home at about five. I live on my own, you see.'

'Then what?' Matthew continued.

'Ummm, well, I had something to eat and then played an online game for a few hours—' Clayton suddenly stopped, giving them each a wide-eye look. 'Do you think I'm honestly the type of person who would hurt Maddy?' he blurted, looking bewilderingly at the detectives.

'You are on record at this school for two sexual harassment complaints against women,' Matthew responded evenly, raising an eyebrow at him. 'I wonder how many other reports could be out there if we went back into your history.'

'I didn't hurt Madeline, I swear,' Clayton stammered. 'I really liked her. I'd never hurt her.'

And Matthew almost believed him.

'Out of curiosity, what online game did you play on Friday night?' Sorenson asked.

Player Beware of Me.

The battle royale game based on hunting people down to shoot and evading being caught was violent, and suddenly the insipid schoolteacher didn't look quite as innocent.

CHAPTER 33: NINA
Friday 17 November

L   *ovelies, I'm coming to Sydney! Dinner at Picolo? Saturday 8pm? Lou xx*

The message came through as Nina was dressing to get ready for the 'end of shoot' party. It was doubling as a farewell gathering as everyone was leaving tomorrow. Some people would be returning to Sydney on Nina and Sassy's flight, whilst others, including Dermott and a couple of the advertising guys were continuing on to Paris for meetings.

Nina's three days in Tahiti had been a tonic, and she didn't know if she was ready to head home just yet. Looking at Louise's text, she felt a warm rush of affection. Her dear friend must have ESP to know that just this minute Nina had needed a reason to get on tomorrow morning's plane.

At least she now had something to look forward to, something much more appealing than attempting to smooth the tension that had been building between her and her husband. Nina was annoyed that David had the gall to be annoyed with her over her insistence that he reimburse her credit card.

'What's the rush? I'll get it to you,' he had grumbled when she had followed him up for the repayment.

'David, you said it would be repaid on Monday,' she had pleaded wearily, and this morning she had finally seen that the amount was now safely back in her bank account. However, there had been no communication from her no doubt sulking husband.

Shrugging off thoughts of David, she added some colourful dangly earrings and the matching beads she had bought at the marketplace and admired the effect they brought to her white halter neck dress. She was normally a pearls girl, but Tahiti brought out the colour in her, and tonight she wanted to embrace it.

A short time later, Nina exited the lift and followed the music to the private patio on the side of the hotel where the Craylee drinks party was set up and the party well underway.

Accepting a glass of the fizz, Nina mingled, chatting with the advertising creative team before peeling off to talk to Dermott.

'Were you happy with how it all went?' she asked, accepting a refill of the delicious wine.

'Absolutely.' He broke out into a radiant grin. 'Everything went off without a hitch. Sassy was sensational. The advertising crew were faultless. And I got to hang out in this beautiful part of the world with people like you.'

Feeling a blush creeping along her face, Nina gave a light laugh. 'Well, I was thrilled to be able to join you all.'

Dermott expanded on his upcoming meetings in France, before he would return to Adelaide, Craylee's headquarters.

'Perhaps when I'm in Sydney next we can catch up again?' he suggested, his eyes boring into hers.

The look was intimate, and Nina felt unsure as to its meaning. She was clearly misreading the signals; after all, her diamond wedding ring was evident as she held the stem of her wineglass. Before she could formulate some sort of reply, he jumped in.

'To meet professionally, of course. Perhaps discuss another project with Sassy?'

His genuine smile had her returning one of her own, feeling relief but in a strange way a sense of disappointment as well.

CHAPTER 34: LOUISE
Saturday 18 November

Louise's head was mulling over her discussions with Matthew just moments before. The close proximity between Central Railways Station where her Canberra bus pulled in and the Surry Hills Police Headquarters had prompted her to arrange the quick drink, and now she was unsure if she wanted to take things further.

It had been great to see Matthew again. He was as easy-going and charismatic as always, with his crinkly eyes and generous smile. He suited the two-tone grey-brown light beard, which was definitely new since she had seen him in Thredbo just weeks before.

'Good to see you, Louise,' Matthew had said, pecking her cheek as she arrived in the dark main bar of his local.

He was still working on the Mount Kosciusko case, and whilst he couldn't share much, he said they were confident of getting a result soon. Louise was relieved to know the nasty perpetrator wouldn't get away with it and gave a momentary shiver, recalling the woman's hand reaching out of the snow.

As for nasty perpetrators, Louise steered the conversation to Anne-Marie's mysterious Henry Dales, who she felt sure was doing his utmost to get one over on her dear friend.

'No criminal record,' had been the first bit of good news voiced by Matthew as they sat hunched over their drinks among a mainly hipster after-work crowd.

'So, he actually exists.' At least that meant he wasn't a Nigerian scammer, which must count for something.

'Yes. He works at Tellus WA Mining in Perth. Some senior executive title, which I have here.' Matthew began to look down at his notes and rattled off the man's long title.

'However.' Matthew looked up warily. 'From what you've said, there's every reason to believe he's still very much married.'

'Why?' Louise asked.

'Because the only address on the database for his vehicle registration is to a large property in Peppermint Grove, and according to my search, he shares that with his wife and children.'

'He could be separated though and living on the property until it's all sorted,' Louise said hopefully.

'Sure. But there's no record of a separation between him and his wife, Lucinda Dales. You said that Anne-Marie hasn't yet met Henry—physically? My theory would be that that's because he's enjoying keeping her and his wife too. I'd warn her about that possibility and see how it pans out.'

****

Louise was the first to arrive at Picolo, one of her favourite restaurants in Sydney because of its relaxed vibe, delicious food and fun cocktail list. Its warm familiarity calmed her as she sat at their regular table and ordered a martini, kicking her overnight bag under the table.

She was already halfway through her cocktail when Nina and Anne-Marie strolled in together laughing.

How could she be the bearer of bad news when they looked so joyful?

An hour of catching up passed, a second bottle of wine was ordered, and their pastas cleared when Louise decided it was now or never.

They had wowed over Nina's photos from Tahiti and even reverted to schoolgirls admiring Mr Craylee, aka Dermott, who Nina had captured in some of the images on her phone.

Louise wished Anne-Marie would fall for someone like him and decided to launch the topic that way. 'Anne-Marie, are you still seeing Henry? Or shall we matchmake Nina's Dermott with you?' Louise gave a teasing smile before gulping a large mouthful of wine.

'Well, I don't know what I'm doing,' Anne-Marie lamented. Her earlier laughter vanished as she shared her aborted plan to surprise him in Perth and her growing frustration that they hadn't yet managed one face-to-face encounter. 'Just one! Is that too much to ask?' Anne-Marie gulped a large mouthful of wine.

Seeing a break in her defences, Louise leapt in. 'Do you worry that maybe he's hiding something?'

'What do you mean?' Anne-Marie asked cautiously, toying with her near-empty wineglass.

'Well, it's been a while now, and let's be honest, what do we really know about him?' She had deliberately used the pronoun in an effort to sound less critical, more supportive, which was something she had found worked for her in her pricklier conversations with Chloe.

Anne-Marie watched her warily, and Louise pressed on. 'I mean, do you think he's been totally honest with who he is, his home life? That sort of thing...'

'Why wouldn't he be?' Anne-Marie snapped, although not as angrily as Louise anticipated, which gave her the confidence to continue.

'Okay. I'm just going to get this out of the way. You remember Matthew, the Queanbeyan detective friend from uni? Well, the thing is, I asked if he could just have a look... you know, just to check Henry's bonafides.'

Anne-Marie's eyes suddenly bulged, but before she could protest, Louise ploughed on.

'There's no easy way to say this, love. I met with Matthew before coming to the restaurant, and well, the thing is, Matthew thinks Henry is married. He said he could delve into it all and find out the real story, but from what I told him, he believed it was typical behaviour for someone leading a double life.'

'He *was* married. I told you that! But he's not now. They're divorced!' Anne-Marie said, flabbergasted. 'I don't understand what you're getting at? And anyway, why would you do that, Louise?' Anne-Marie looked at her in disbelief.

'Because I was worried about you, love. Come on, it's been more than four months now and he's still a mystery man you've never met. I'm worried that he's stringing you along and enjoying having the best of both worlds. I don't want you to get hurt,' she said, hoping to smooth over the hurt.

'How could you?' Anne-Marie blustered, pushing her seat back noisily. 'We love each other! You are just jealous. Both of you! You just want to keep me pathetically single.'

With that, Anne-Marie stood up and pulled out some notes to leave for the bill before storming away and into the night, leaving more than two dazed diners in her wake.

CHAPTER 35: MATTHEW

Matthew collapsed heavily in one of the two large armchairs in the sparsely furnished serviced apartment that was his temporary home in Sydney. His head swam from the booze he had consumed over the past few hours, and his body slumped like a dead weight, immovable.

Devens had insisted the team down a few beers at Stevo's pub together and take a rest day on Sunday.

'You've all put in the hard yards, so stay on and have at least one more drink on me. We'll regroup on Monday at nine sharp.' Their chief placed a fifty-dollar note on the bar and disappeared into the night. It was more than enough for another round of beers and shots for Sorenson, Davies and Matthew.

It had been a night to let off steam, recalibrate and now sleep—something he hadn't had much of since getting to Sydney a week ago.

Matthew's eyes began to close before he remembered his phone and reached for it.

He wanted to see if he had missed any calls in the noisy pub, but the screen remained surprisingly blank.

If nothing else, he expected a message from Louise. She was planning to talk to Anne-Marie this evening, and he had promised to be on standby for a coffee meeting on Sunday, if Anne-Marie wanted to take things further.

Louise's friend seemed a force to be reckoned with, so he was glad it wasn't him delivering the news. He couldn't imagine her taking it well.

Sweet Louise, she was such a softy at heart. Anyway, he might hear from her tomorrow and catch up with the brittle Anne-Marie but only as a favour to his old university mate.

With absolutely no one needing him, he let his eyelids droop and fell asleep in seconds.

****

When Matthew awoke the next morning, he felt stiff and sore from sleeping in the armchair all night. He should have forced himself to go to bed.

Staggering to his feet, he stretched his neck and shoulders and went to the bedroom to change out of last night's clothes.

Fifteen minutes later, he was taking in the sights of his new neighbourhood as it came to life early on a Sunday morning. NSW Police had put him in a serviced apartment at Broadway, not too far from the police headquarters, which made for an easy daily commute by foot.

Today, however, he ventured in the opposite direction, down towards Prince Alfred Park. The green space was a sanctuary in the otherwise concrete jungle he was living in, and he filled his lungs hungrily as he began his run.

After notching up six kilometres around the park and beyond, he slowed his pace to a walk and eventually stopped to pick up fresh bagels and the weekend newspapers.

The Madeline Bright case wasn't in today's rag, and he could understand why. Developments had been slow, so there really wasn't anything new to say.

Later, freshly showered and sitting at the dining table with a Nespresso coffee and a smoked salmon and cream cheese bagel, he flicked open Maddy's file. He wanted to look at it all again. See what they were missing. There had to be something…

CHAPTER 36: ANNE-MARIE
Sunday 19 November

Anne-Marie was on her third lap of Centennial Park, and the endorphins were kicking in nicely now that she was fifteen kilometres into her bike ride. She had needed the mental shift, not to mention an outlet to work off the fury still gripping her.

Bloody Louise had no right to pry into Henry. How dare she! The indignity flared again, just thinking about it. Her perfect Henry picked to pieces by Louise and that stupid bloody detective. What would he know? How dare he insinuate Henry was a fraud, leading her along. That she was so stupid she would have fallen for someone who was still married. Henry was legitimate! Of course he was.

And even if he was still married, she wasn't doing anything wrong. She was a free agent. Although she had been down that road before and this time wasn't prepared to be a mistress. She wanted the whole thing. She had dated two married men before and knew that leaving wives had never been on the cards for either of them. With them, she hadn't minded. It had suited them both. But with Henry, she had mapped out her whole future. Would she confront him? Give him an ultimatum?

Her thoughts had been swirling all night, which was how she found herself here on a Sunday morning with the rest of the eastern suburbs weekend cycling fraternity, looping the park to gulp in fresh air and work off some energy.

Anne-Marie kept a lookout for Hellie and Barbs, two of her cycling mates, but couldn't see them among the fluoro shapes cycling by. She should have texted them that she was going to be here after all. But that only served to remind her of why she hadn't arranged to meet up in the first place. Henry of course! She had cancelled her regular Sunday ride/breakfast with them to pay him a surprise visit in Perth… before he had dropped his Dubai bombshell text.

Maybe Louise had a point. What did she really know about Henry other than what he had shared over the phone and in his emails? But surely you only knew as much as a person wanted to reveal. It didn't mean they were duplicitous. But she had experienced a niggle or two, hadn't she? If she was being honest with herself, it had been at least a month now that she had started questioning things.

Pulling off the path and slowing down near the café, she wondered if Louise had just been telling her what she had known all along? There was something slightly iffy about this seemingly perfect man. But if that was the case, then everything she'd done for the past four months was such a waste, not to mention humiliating. She had invested precious time (and money) on a married man. And married men never leave their wives, at least in her experience.

Getting off the bike and leaning it against a wall, she removed her helmet and queued for a coffee. As she waited, she felt her fingers automatically reach for her mobile. She had ignored last night's concerned messages from Louise and Nina, but now scanned them again.

Sorry to meddle. Just worried you might get hurt. Love you heaps. Lou xx

Anne-Marie, hope you're okay? Call me if you want to chat? Nina x

After ordering her takeaway, she pressed Louise's number.

'Anne-Marie?' Louise said eagerly.

'Wow, that was fast.' Anne-Marie was caught off guard because the phone hadn't even begun to ring through.

'Oh, Anne-Marie. It's so good to hear from you. I was just about to call you. I had my phone in my hand.'

'Really?'

'I'm so sorry, love. I just don't know what I was thinking. But I only wanted to look out for you.'

'It's okay, Lou.' Anne-Marie felt guilty at hearing the upset in Louise's voice. 'I understand why you did what you did.'

Sighing, Anne-Marie said, 'If I'm honest, I've been wondering myself if Henry's too good to be true. Although I bloody hope not!' She let out a light laugh. 'I've spent a shitload of time and money on this relationship.'

'Money?' Louise said, sounding alarmed.

'Oh, well, not really. Well… not much… just a small amount… but anyway.' She fumbled, not wanting to alarm Louise further.

'Hi, Anne-Marie.' Nina's voice sounded in the background.

'I'll put you on speaker,' Louise announced, and suddenly background noise filled her ear.

'Are you okay, love?' Nina's voice sounded worried, and Anne-Marie regretted her abrupt departure from what had been a lovely dinner together last night.

'Yeah, sorry to be an idiot last night,' Anne-Marie said, rolling her eyes even though her friends couldn't see her.

'Hey, it's okay. I'm sorry I upset you,' Louise said.

'What do you think you'll do?' Nina asked.

'I really don't know,' Anne-Marie said glumly. Her coffee order was just then called out by the barista, and she walked over to fetch it, all the while listening as her girlfriends hatched a plan.

CHAPTER 37: MATTHEW

Matthew arrived at the swanky address punctually at two and pressed the buzzer.

'Hello?' a cheery female voice sounded.

'It's Matthew,' he replied before being buzzed in.

Walking up the stairs and towards the open apartment door, he was greeted by Louise.

'Like your digs,' he remarked, kissing her on the cheek.

'I wish!' Louise laughed.

'Come on in,' a voice called out, and he instantly recognised Nina from their encounter at Mount Kosciusko.

The enormous apartment had a breathtaking view over Bronte Beach and occupied the entire level of the three-story building. He followed them to the outside deck to admire the sparkling ocean.

'David and I bought out the other two apartment owners and made it one,' Nina said. 'I just love it here. Anyway, come back inside and I'll get you something to drink.'

He followed the women into the living room and noticed Anne-Marie sitting quietly. She was curled up in the corner of the enormous grey sofa, almost obscured by the myriad of cushions around her. The confidence and fiery temperament he recalled from first meeting her was now muted. She didn't look up.

'Anne-Marie, you remember Matthew?' Louise prompted.

'Hi,' Anne-Marie murmured, not quite meeting Matthew's eye and sounding as moody as he recalled.

'Good to see you all again,' he said casually at her half-turned face, before glancing at Nina and Louise, who were giving him encouraging smiles. A flicker of worry went through him as he watched Anne-Marie try to slide even further into the corner of the L-shaped sofa as if she would rather be anywhere but in this room. A decorative cushion was thrust in front of her like a protective shield.

'So, I'm going to put some tea and coffee on and leave you guys to chat,' Nina said merrily, ignoring the obvious tension in the room.

Matthew and Louise sat down on the armchairs opposite Anne-Marie, and he looked over to see if Louise was going to kick things off. Instead, he was met with an eye-roll before Louise's head bent exaggeratedly from Anne-Marie to him, silently pleading for him to begin.

Clearing his throat, Matthew began. 'Anne-Marie, I gather Louise filled you in on our catch-up?'

'Mmm,' she replied, fingering the tassels on the cushion.

'Did you want me to repeat anything we discussed?'

'No, it's fine,' she replied crisply. 'I already know you think he's still married.'

'Would you like me to delve deeper into this matter?' he asked and was finally rewarded with her direct gaze.

Anne-Marie's worried brown eyes sought his, and he could see a flood of uncertainty pass through them as she appeared to weigh up his offer. The hurt was plain to see, so too her vulnerability and fear.

'What would that entail?' she asked cautiously.

As Nina poured out coffees and placed a mince tart on each plate, Matthew explained that one avenue could be to have a private investigator follow Henry for a few days and establish whether he was, in fact, living the life of a doting husband and father. Confirm that his marital status was intact.

'Or you could ask him yourself?' Matthew said.

'But then he'd know that I was suspicious,' Anne-Marie snapped. 'He would think I've been snooping. That I don't trust him!'

'But we don't trust him!' Louise blurted, and Matthew watched Anne-Marie's head swivel instantly to glare at her.

'I didn't say that, Louise. You've never liked him. Just admit it!' Anne-Marie was clearly annoyed, and Matthew leapt in before things escalated.

'Hey, guys. Let's stick to the facts. We've established a home address and workplace. We can tail him and see what his lifestyle is about and whether it's separate from that of his family or if it isn't. That way you will at least know what the situation is.'

'Why don't you do that, Anne-Marie?' said Nina gently, now perched on the sofa armrest.

'No. Just leave it.' Anne-Marie shook her head. 'I don't want to do that to Henry. He's my soul mate, and if he said they're divorced, then I believe him.'

Matthew looked over at Louise, who rolled her eyes again but was smart enough not to add anything further.

'Okay then. But if you change your mind, Louise has my details. In fact, I'll give you my card as well.'

Matthew pulled out a business card from his wallet and slid it over to Anne-Marie.

After finishing his coffee, he said goodbye to the three women. He left feeling that he had achieved very little.

CHAPTER 38: NINA

Nina's husband had been scarcely home all weekend, but then neither had she, hanging out at Anne-Marie's for much of the past twenty-four hours. She couldn't exactly complain that he was ignoring her, because he might have accused her of the same thing. And he would be right.

David had played eighteen holes of golf yesterday and was in a club tournament today, something he always took very seriously, such was his competitive nature. He was probably now celebrating at the nineteenth hole, and she didn't expect to see him until much later tonight.

Sunday nights always made Nina melancholy. Perhaps the years of boarding school and being shut back in for the whole week. She knew Anne-Marie felt the same way; they had both been boarders at Saint Augustine's, Rose Bay, over thirty years ago, but the depressing memories remained ingrained. A fun-filled day out on Sunday, flirting with the private school boys at a pub they shouldn't have been able to get into, only to hastily scramble back inside the school gates within seconds of the eight o'clock curfew. The excitement would be over for another week, replaced by strict discipline, isolation and tedious monotony.

Her mind now wandered back to the final night in Tahiti where she had felt so happy and carefree. It was like ten years or more had been erased when she had been dancing the night away and downing shots of tequila with Sassy and the film crew. And Dermott of course. She blushed thinking about him and the slow dance they had enjoyed on the lawn. Just them. God how she was tempted and how disappointed she was when the night came to an end and Dermott escorted her back to her room.

What could have been if she had given in to her desire and invited him in.

Feeling the blush deepen, Nina decided to busy herself with Anne-Marie's woes. Picking up her mobile, she dialled her number.

'I feel like an idiot,' Anne-Marie groaned. 'I lost it again today with you guys, didn't I?'

'Hey, don't beat yourself up. We can take it.' Nina gave a light laugh, reflecting on all the tiffs they had resolved over the years. Their spats never amounted to any permanent damage.

'I just want to give Henry the benefit of the doubt, but Louise is just so convinced that he's doing the dirty on his wife. If they're still living under the same roof, it's platonic. I'm sure of it,' Anne-Marie said confidently.

Nina had a glimmer of understanding. If she could trade David for Dermott, wouldn't she?

Keen to get off the dangerous topic of unhappy marriages and marital affairs, Nina segued into the latest Netflix drama she was watching about four friends, and their conversation shifted easily.

By the time she disconnected the call, Nina felt lighter from the silly laughs she had shared with Anne-

Marie. The awful hour of eight o'clock had slipped by now.

David still hadn't arrived home, but she didn't mind. She reached for the TV remote to find some of the viewing options Anne-Marie had just mentioned.

CHAPTER 39: MATTHEW
Monday 20 November

Devens had agreed with Matthew that the schoolteacher was worth pinning up on the board as a potential suspect. Clayton Jones had form—the two sexual harassment complaints in his file at Blue Leaf Public School—and he also appeared to enjoy violence, based on his online gaming.

However, in the days since they had spoken to Clayton, Matthew just couldn't see how the teacher could have done it within the time frame. He was on-site at the primary school at seven thirty sharp on Friday 3 November, the morning Maddy was last seen, and he hadn't left the premises until 5:10 p.m. His movements had been verified by the school log-in system and other witness statements from staff at the school.

The tech team had also obtained information off Clayton's laptop to show that he was, in fact, playing the video game until late Friday night. And his movements for both Saturday and Sunday had also been independently verified through a combination of receipts, CCTV footage and witness accounts.

Sorenson had also spoken with the two women who had lodged internal complaints against Clayton Jones and had come away with very little.

The P&C member Beverley Taellow had told Sorenson that it had all just been a "silly misunderstanding", "a little harmless flirting gone wrong" was how she had described it.

'Beverley Taellow blames herself for drinking too much and said that what had started as playful flirting at the school function ended up going too far. I gather a lewd text was intercepted by her husband, and she felt pressured to make a complaint to the school,' said Sorenson. 'Anyway, she said she later withdrew her complaint when she realised the damage it could do to Clayton's career.'

As for the supply teacher Katie Allowster, she said Clayton Jones had cornered her outside the school in the car park when she was leaving late one evening and made suggestive comments to her. But that was the extent of it.

'Both women described him as being fixated and odd, but neither viewed him as a violent type. Just weird and inappropriate,' Sorenson said in summary.

'Okay, troops. We'll keep the teacher up there for now,' said Devens, tapping Clayton Jones's photo on the whiteboard. 'But let's go back to what we actually have. And more importantly, what are we missing?'

Matthew spoke up. 'I reckon the focus should be on Maddy's boyfriend and his flatmate, Moses.'

The team waited as Matthew walked over to the board and pointed at the timeline.

'Look, Maddy was last sighted by Jake when he kissed her goodbye before leaving for work early on Friday morning—which we only have his word for.

According to the flatmate'—Matthew singled out Moses's headshot—'he never saw Maddy that morning. Again, we only have his word for that. What we do know is that Maddy's last movements have been traced to being in the northern beaches flat. There have been no sightings since. One of these two men knows something.'

Devens nodded. 'Okay. Let's put the pressure on and see if we can get them talking. I'll make an order to the Supreme Court for a listening device so we can bug the flat and see what the flatmates have to say. We'll also extend the warrant to both men's mobile phones.

'In the meantime, Davies, I want you to drill down into every hour of Jake's movements that weekend. We need more than what we have right now, and if you can't get it corroborated, look into CCTV, receipts, whatever. That means go to the gym he said he visited on Friday afternoon. Speak to the manager, and see what time he did get there—after all, he would most likely need to swipe in.'

'Matthew, likewise, with Moses. We want to get anything that has them heading south to Thredbo that weekend. And I mean anything.'

****

The next morning the team regrouped to go through what they had found.

Davies, who had been assigned Jake, began; 'So the boyfriend has told us that he left the apartment for work at six-fifteen on Friday morning. According to him, Maddy was going to take a shower in the shared bathroom when he left the flat. But that's not verified by Moses or anyone else, at least not yet.'

Jake's presence at the Seaforth building site all day had been corroborated by the builder's crew of six workers, said Davies.

'Jake said he got home from work around four and went to the gym from five thirty to seven, but none of this can be verified,' Davies said. 'There's no security swipe system at his club, and so far, I've had conflicting accounts from witnesses there—a manager and a PT.'

Jake's movements that night were that he picked up a takeaway, went home and watched the National Basketball League late with Moses—where their mutual alibi slipped in. *Convenient,* thought Matthew.

'Jake's movements on Saturday are more watertight, rugby training at nine before a three-o'clock game at Bowral and partying in Manly until the wee hours at Stellars' nightclub with his teammates. Numerous witness statements support the version of events.'

Why he didn't phone or text his girlfriend all weekend still rankled Matthew, and he made a note to find out more before updating the team on Moses.

'Moses said that he slept late on Friday and called in sick. The receptionist at the plumbing company where he works, WeWork, has confirmed receiving a phone message from him at eight. He claimed to have eventually got up at lunchtime on Friday and surfed all day at Avalon and Mona Vale before having a few quiet beers on the beach and getting home around ten, when he joined Jake on the sofa to watch NBL until around eleven or twelve. All pretty vague,' commented Matthew. 'We haven't found anyone to substantiate Moses's account of where he was on Friday all day and evening, except from Jake, who said Moses was at the flat that night.' His mobile phone was eerily silent all day, so it provided few clues.

Saturday had been a different story. Moses was a winger on the Seagulls rugby team, and together with Jake and at least fifteen others, his movements had been accounted for all day and night on Saturday.

'Keep drilling,' Devens instructed. 'Let's get a tighter timeline for Moses and Jake. They've both alibied each other to some degree, but I want their timelines under a microscope. Minute by minute.'

'Davies, check tollways, cameras, et cetera, for either vehicle. If one of them was driving south, we need to find it.'

'Do either of them smoke?' Sorenson asked.

'They say not, but let's see if the cigarette butts tell us otherwise when we eventually get the DNA,' said Devens.

Devens continued to dispense jobs for the day, and Matthew's assignment was to examine both men's social media feeds, especially during the forty-eight-hour period from Friday morning to Sunday morning when Maddy's body had been discovered.

Matthew clicked the mouse on his computer and brought up Facebook. He was sure one of them would have a profile, and it didn't take long to find it. Bingo. Moses did.

There in all his technicolour glory was Moses, grinning at the screen with a lazy arm hung over his bestie, both looking wasted. The date—Saturday 4 November—the venue, Stellars.

Matthew spent the afternoon looking back into the social media pages of Moses Galvin, not only to see what else he might have posted but also to study his timeline. It niggled him that Moses had the same months every year unaccounted for with paid plumbing work, and he wanted to establish what Moses did during the months of July to September when his résumé was devoid of plumbing contracts.

It didn't take long. Within twenty minutes, Matthew's screen was alive with evidence of exactly how Moses spent his winter months. Snowboarding. The image of a delighted Moses with a GoPro fixed on his helmet, beaming at the camera, was followed by at least a dozen or more other photos and videos of the avid board rider in action. The dates of the posts were dotted with days in July, August and early September of this year.

So, he knows the mountain well, thought Matthew, printing out the images to show Devens.

That's interesting, very interesting indeed.

CHAPTER 40: LOUISE

The shop was hers! Louise couldn't believe how fast it had been to turn her long-held dream into a reality.

Just last week she had been finalising her business plan with Theodore and her accountant, and today the bank manager had given her the green light.

The manager had approved a business loan without much fanfare, as if it was all perfectly normal to want to borrow $100,000 to invest in this new venture. The amount scared Louise at first, but it would be worth it because within twelve months she would be returning a tidy profit from the workshop program and "artist in residence" studio series.

Some of the bank loan would be used for a minor refurbishment to the shop, which hadn't seen much love in the past few years. Louise had already consulted a builder and planned to remove some of the bulky grey fixtures and create a light-filled contemporary studio space that would be freshly painted in off-white. Money would also be invested in buying two or maybe even three long whitewashed timber workbenches and stools for each, and Louise felt excited imagining the room filled with eager students. She would also acquire tools and supplies for the classes, including an assortment of pliers, wire and wire cutters and dazzling beads.

Another twenty-four hours later and Louise was leaving the realtor's office with the contract for the shopfront. A three-year lease giving her all the time in the world to turn her vision into a profitable reality.

It was all so exciting!

Louise had to restrain herself from dancing down the street when she left the agency and instead hurriedly walked to her favourite café to celebrate with a pot of English Breakfast tea and decadent chocolate éclair. *So much for my diet!*

Tomorrow she would meet with the builder and finalise her plans for the space. Then she was going to start reaching out to the long list of jewellers and artists she wanted to schedule to showcase their talents and designs. But right now she was going to take this moment to savour the start of something and the sweet treat in front of her.

Hi will visit 2nite xx pinged a text from Chloe.

Wow, could her day get any better? Her absent daughter was going to come home for dinner this evening. Refilling her cup with the steaming black tea, she pulled out her notepad to sketch out a schedule of art classes, workshops and seminars. She couldn't wait to get started.

CHAPTER 41: ANNE-MARIE
Wednesday 22 November

Nina had suggested a rare lunch together in the city, and Anne-Marie was grateful for the distraction.

For three days now Anne-Marie had been fretfully anticipating a call or at least a text from Henry but had heard nothing. She was actually relieved in a way because she wasn't sure how she would bring up his marital status.

Perhaps it was best to await his return from Dubai. Henry often went quiet when he was travelling with work, juggling time zones, early meetings, late dinners, that type of thing.

No, right now she needed to be patient and bide her time.

At one-o'clock-sharp Anne-Marie entered Bellinis, an Italian café that was just a couple of blocks from her corporate travel office and not too far from Martin Place, where Nina worked.

Despite being so close, they rarely met up during the workday as both were usually tied to their desks or committed to meetings, corporate lunches or interstate travel.

Anne-Marie ordered a skinny cap and reviewed the lunch menu whilst she waited for Nina to arrive. Her eyes lit up at the Wagyu beef burger and fries, but she forced her gaze across to the other side of the menu to the various salad options and selected the kale and cranberries with fresh lemon dressing.

'Sorry I'm late.' Nina leant in for a half embrace before sitting down and unloading her enormous black Chanel handbag on the spare chair beside her. It was classy enough to warrant its own seat at the table, unlike Anne-Marie's tatty leather over-the-shoulder bag that sat forlornly under the table like a loyal pet.

After ordering a large bottle of mineral water and their salads, Nina alluded to the reason she wanted to meet. 'I wanted to suggest a little matchmaking.' Her eyes were alight with excitement.

Anne-Marie looked at her, puzzled. She didn't understand who Nina was looking to matchmake, but then the penny dropped. Well, more like thudded, but before Anne-Marie could protest, Nina pushed on.

'You know that lovely man I met in Tahiti?' Nina gushed enthusiastically.

'The champagne executive?' Anne-Marie asked warily.

'Yes! Dermott Sage. Well, he's been in touch. He's visiting from Adelaide next week, and I wanted to see if you would like me to arrange a date? Nothing too serious. Just a drink after work? He's really lovely, and I'm sure you'd really like him.'

Anne-Marie knew Nina's heart was as big as the ocean, but she couldn't go on a random date with a "nice man" when Henry was still very much the one she wanted to be with.

'I haven't given up on Henry,' she said, giving Nina a small smile.

'But Anne-Marie, what if he really is married?'

'We don't know that for sure... and, if even he is, well so be it. I'm not.' She shrugged, taking a sip of her drink.

Now it was Nina's turn to look puzzled, her face scrunching up in worry. However, Anne-Marie had given this a lot of thought. If Henry's marriage was dead, like he said it was, then what was stopping them from being together?

Over their kale and cranberries, Anne-Marie expanded on her rationale, but Nina was unusually opinionated about the topic.

'Marriage is a *vow*, Anne-Marie. Surely you owe it to Henry and his wife to try to sort it out first before anything progresses with you two?'

'But we're already involved, Nins. I love him. I really do.'

'Are you sure you just don't love what he represents?' Nina cautioned. 'You know. Freedom. Romance. Escapism...' Nina's voice drifted off. She looked wistful, and Anne-Marie began to wonder if they were still talking about Henry. Nina returned her attention to her. 'Anyway. I just wanted to put out another prospect to think about.'

'Thanks for looking out for me. I really appreciate it. But I just want to give Henry the benefit of the doubt. If he's "technically" still married, it will be in name only,' Anne-Marie said, confident that she and Henry could work through this minor obstacle and map out a suitable timeline for them to be together.

'I just don't want you to be misled. Hurt,' Nina soothed.

'I won't. I promise,' Anne-Marie said reassuringly, because Henry's love was the real deal.

CHAPTER 42: MATTHEW
Friday 24 November

The social media images of Moses at Thredbo had rung alarm bells in Matthew's head.

It was too much of a coincidence that Madeline Bright's body had been found on the same mountain that Moses had skied on. In fact, too coincidental to be a coincidence.

Matthew studied the images over the past few days, searching for something that might present a lead. And then he saw it. A discrete logo on the right side of a ski jacket in one of the images. It wasn't being worn by Moses but by another man who was standing in one of the photographs.

Matthew opened up the Mountain Ski Resort website and Facebook pages and began scrolling through the hundreds of images. He had a hunch the thirty-year-old had a seasonal job at the snow, which would explain how Moses spent his winter months without earning money as a Sydney plumber.

And bingo, there Moses was, captured in one of the ski company's official photos, instructing a group of young people on snowboarding.

Matthew would bet his life on Moses's being a regular for the past few years, and therefore he would know every inch of Thredbo, including fire trails such as the one that had been used to dump Maddy's body.

Now he just needed to find some evidence.

****

The listening device had been installed whilst Jake and Moses were at work, and it had been a few days now without anything forthcoming.

'Okay, listen up. This is what we are going to do,' commanded Devens, rallying the team together in the office on Friday afternoon. It was now three weeks, and they had little to show for their efforts. Matthew knew first-hand how hard it was to keep spirits up when progress was slow.

'Davies, I want you to phone Jake tomorrow morning when we know he'll be at home. Make it early, no later than eight, before he heads to rugby practice and then his afternoon game. Request the pleasure of his company on Monday afternoon at four, after work, to answer a few more questions.'

That would mean Jake would have all weekend to think about the meeting and potentially discuss it with Moses. At least that is what they were hoping.

'It would be good to flag that we are revisiting the timeline for Madeline's disappearance,' suggested Matthew. 'It could get them talking about their alibis.'
'Yes. Let's see what transpires over the weekend, and we can then take a crack at Moses next week,' Devens agreed. 'If our suspicions are correct, we should hear some worthwhile chatter going on this weekend, which will give us more to talk about with the flatmates early next week.'

CHAPTER 43: LOUISE
Saturday 25 November

New Age Jewels had a flurry of shoppers since Louise opened up at ten, and four hours later it had quietened down enough for Chloe to dash off and fetch them a late lunch of mini quiches and sodas.

Saturdays were always busy, and with her regular assistant away at a wedding, Louise was grateful to have her daughter on hand. It reminded her of the fun times when Chloe had been a lot more involved in the jewellery shop, helping out after school and each Saturday. Perhaps they could work out a new arrangement for Chloe in the business? Especially with Louise's expansion plans.

Although when Louise had shared her plans with Chloe over dinner earlier that week, her daughter hadn't been quite as enthusiastic as she had anticipated. But then again, Chloe had looked tired and on edge.

'Why would you want to do that, Mum?' Chloe had queried when Louise had expanded on her plans for the jewellery classes and events she wanted to host in the new space.

'It's always been a dream of your mother's,' Theodore had explained gently. 'I think it's marvellous!'

Good on Theodore for always having her back. Excitedly embracing her vision.

Chloe had instead responded with, 'Oh, okay, I guess…' as if she still wasn't entirely convinced, let alone interested in the direction Louise was taking New Age Jewels. However before Louise could wow her with the many other thoughts she had for her workshops, Chloe had changed the topic, steering Theodore's attention to some paperwork that she wanted him to review. Something related to her work and wages.

'What's that all about?' Louise had asked as she stirred the risotto, but their heads were buried over the documents, and she was effectively cut out of whatever was so much more enthralling than New Age Jewels and all the things Louise had planned. Well, at least whatever it was had brought her daughter home for an evening meal, which Chloe seriously needed, judging by her skinny frame. As a family they hadn't sat down together for dinner for months, so she would be grateful for that. Clearly Chloe was just super busy right now and no doubt tired with her late shifts at the night club. That's all it was, Louise reassured herself, watching Theodore refill Chloe and his wineglasses.

****

'Here you go,' Chloe said, handing over the warm paper bag and napkin to Louise, before pulling out a small bottle of iced tea from her handbag. 'And your drink.'

'Oh, and I've got your change in here.' Chloe began to fumble in the bottom of her bag, but Louise waved her off.

'You keep it.' She smiled across at her adorable daughter.

'Thanks, Mum.' Chloe smiled, a genuine sweetness in her eyes, and Louise's heart melted. She missed those endearing exchanges.

Louise had already promised to pay Chloe handsomely for working today, but it was worth it just to hang out with her beautiful girl. Although right now she wasn't looking her sparkling best. Her usually clear skin showed signs of breakouts, and her hair was limp and looked in need of a good shampoo.

She would talk to her about looking after herself with good sleep, exercise and healthy food and cutting back on the partying. But not now. She didn't want to ruin this moment by transforming into "nagging Mum".

So, biting her tongue, Louise gave her a bright smile. 'I'll just pop out the back to chomp into this love if you just keep an eye on things?'

Disappearing into her office, Louise unwrapped the quiche and took a mouthful. She could hear the light filter of conversation on the floor and glowed inwardly.

'Oh yes, they are perfect for you,' Chloe schmoozed one of the shoppers who had been browsing a row of dangly art deco earrings for the past half an hour.

'Do you really think so?' the woman asked anxiously.

'Absolutely. Let me get the bigger mirror.'

Yep, Chloe was a natural at charming people, Louise thought fondly, knowing her daughter had just the same effect on her.

Perhaps she would spring for them to have a mother/daughter treatment at her hair salon next week? Chloe would like that!

CHAPTER 44: NINA

David had been slamming drawers in his home office all morning, and a loud clang sounded as he dropped the phone handset heavily into its cradle. It was supposed to be a quiet Sunday afternoon at home, and Nina had had enough.

'What's going on?' she demanded, marching into their home office, which looked like a mini tornado had ripped through it. The usually tidy desk was covered in a mound of paperwork with several chequebooks and bank statements peeping out from under the rubble.

'The bloody mongrels won't play ball!' David snapped, stabbing at his keyboard impatiently.

'Who?' she asked, baffled.

David just shook his head before shutting his laptop.

'It's just work stuff. I'll sort it out tomorrow.' He began to shuffle the files and loose paper into piles.

Relieved it wasn't anything to do with their personal financials yet not wanting to know anything more about the perilous state of his business affairs, Nina didn't comment or enquire.

'Work is really full on of late,' Nina remarked, worried about the strain it was taking on David. 'Well, at least there's Aspen to look forward to.' She was trying to lift his spirits and defuse the tension emanating from the room, but instead David looked up at her like a deer in the headlights. 'Skiing. Christmas?' she prompted, whilst he stared at her blankly.

At David's insistence a few months back, Nina had booked a two-week Colorado vacation for them. It seemed more important than ever now, as she and David were in dire need of reconnecting and spending some quality time together away from all their stress of work—especially his. David hadn't been himself for months, and a widening rift was emerging between them.

'Of course!' David suddenly rebounded, giving her a wink. 'I'll just finish up here and be out shortly.'
As Nina walked back to the kitchen, one more seed of worry began to grow.

CHAPTER 45: MATTHEW

As anticipated, the police bug began to sing.

It wasn't long after Davies had made the telephone call to Jake on Saturday morning that the first conversation about the case materialised.

Moses and Jake were in the kitchen, making breakfast before leaving for rugby practice, when Jake mentioned the police had just phoned to ask him to go back into the station.

'They want me to help them with a few more questions for their investigation.' Jake sounded puzzled.

'Seriously?' Moses said sharply. 'Did they say what they want to talk to you about?'

'Nah. Just to go in on Monday after work. Weird, hey. I don't know what else I can tell them.'

'Just keep it short and sweet mate, hey,' Moses said.

The topic was then dropped, and the audio filled with the sounds of an active kitchen, chairs scraping, cutlery and plates tinkering and the jug boiling.

However, the next evening the detectives found the flatmates' conversation a whole lot more interesting.

'Hey, mate. Just thinking about your catch-up with the cops tomorrow,' Moses started casually.

'Yeah.' Jake's mumble was quiet over the television blaring with what sounded like the Sunday rugby league match of the day.

'Yeah, mate. What do you reckon they want to talk to you about?'

'Dunno,' Jake said, nonplussed.

'Did they say?'

'No, just usual stuff, you know... Help them find out what happened, tell them some more about Maddy so they can find out the fuckwit who did this. Check timelines—'

'Timelines?' Moses interjected.

'Yeah, you know. Where I was that weekend. That sort of thing.'

There was a pause for ten minutes or so as booming sports commentary was heard over the bug before the men's talk resumed.

'Hey, mate. Let's just get your story straight, hey,' Moses said with determination. 'I mean you haven't done anything wrong, mate, but you know what coppers are like. Trying to trip people up. Turn words around, that sort of thing, hey.'

'What do you mean?'

'Well, like we already told them, right? Friday night we were both here watching television. You know, the NBL.'

'Yeah, sure. I know.'

'Right, so I was here by ten tops. Okay?' Moses said forcefully.

'Sure, mate,' Jake replied more quietly. 'What difference does it make if it ended up being later anyway?'

'No, ten o'clock I was here, right? Maybe even earlier? Say nine... no, leave it at ten as we don't want to start mucking around with what we already told them.' Moses's voice had a slight edge to it.

'Yeah,' Jake reassured him, before asking, 'Where were you anyway? You know. Beforehand.'

'Just doing stuff,' Moses said dismissively. 'Like you, hey mate? With that sexy client.'

'Oh piss off!' Jake laughed.

'Yeah, you didn't think I said anything though, did you? Gym my ass, mate. I know you and *Mrs Seaforth* were going at it like rabbits. But I'm not going to tell anyone, hey. Least of all that prick of a client of yours! And certainly not the police. It's what *mates* do, isn't it? Hey?'

'Yeah, mate. We're all good,' Jake said before the conversation was dropped and loud cheering from the television filled the void.

'Sounds like young Jake might have a bit on the side,' Davies commented, raising his eyebrows suggestively as Devens stopped the recording.

'I'd hazard a guess that those early and late meetings with the "client" on the building site didn't have anything to do with going through spreadsheets,' Davies continued, earning an eye-roll from Sorenson, who had little tolerance for Davies's sometimes laddish comments.

'Let's talk to the woman concerned,' said Devens, nodding at Davies.

'On it, sir.' Davies smirked.

CHAPTER 46: NINA
Monday 27 November

After a night spent tossing and turning, Nina made an urgent appointment with her accountant, Miles Jeffries.

David's financial stress was worrying her, and she wanted reassurance from Miles that her business affairs and their personal finances were shipshape.

If David's business suddenly went belly up, she needed to know they were protected. The niggle she had been feeling for some time was now becoming difficult to ignore.

Nina took two ibuprofen, fetched the latest folder of financial statements from her desk and raced out to her waiting taxi, willing the tension headache to fade before it was time to pore over numbers with Miles.

'So, as I said on the phone, Nina, it's all a tad unusual,' began her fatherly accountant fifteen minutes later. 'It's unorthodox to be frank. There's the $22,000 debt on the Talent Time credit card, which I understand David has now reimbursed?'

Nina nodded mutely.

'However, I'm afraid that's the least of it.' Her accountant sounded grim, which exacerbated her headache.

Nina had carved out an hour in her busy afternoon for reassurance, but it didn't look like she would be getting any.

'As requested, I've looked into all your accounts—both Talent Time and personal—and I can see a few other discrepancies. There's $186,000 of withdrawals from your Reserve account, which is the account that I instructed to have on standby for any necessary emergencies such as unexpected expenses or additional taxes. Plus there's a loan out on your personal property in Bronte, which we should have known about as that's all tied in with the business finance.'

What loan on their Bronte home? Nina's pulse quickened as she moved to the edge of her seat, listening to more details on the dire state of her finances.

'I'll need a few days to untangle the web, but I anticipate a serious cash flow problem if we don't halt any further outgoing loans and significant payments,' Miles warned.

'I'd also like you to apply for an overdraft account immediately for Talent Time. I fear there may be some lean months ahead, and with payroll and business costs, you will need access to ready funds. I'm not sure if you were planning on Christmas bonuses this year?' he asked, looking at her with a grimace. 'Perhaps hold off until I get a proper handle on things.'

Nina couldn't speak, as tears welled in her eyes. How could she let her business become so vulnerable? How could her husband have put them in this perilous financial position?

CHAPTER 47: MATTHEW

Jake looked visibly shaken and unsure as he stumbled through his answers early on Monday afternoon.

Matthew and Devens took their time to prompt him through his movements on Friday 3 November, and this seemed to unsettle Jake even more.

'Just going back to the last time you saw Madeline. We understand this was around six-fifteen on Friday morning before you set off to Seaforth to the building site?' Devens stated.

'Yes,' Jake replied.

'And then you didn't speak to Maddy *all weekend?*' Matthew asked.

He had gone through the phone records for Maddy, Jake and Moses, which confirmed there had been no calls or texts with Maddy.

'No. I had stuff on,' he mumbled.

'We asked you earlier how things were between you both. And we're now asking you again. Please think about this before you answer this time. It doesn't matter how big or small it was. Were you and Madeline fighting before her disappearance? Did you have an argument? Big or small,' Devens asked.

Jake gulped before nodding, looking down at the table.

'So, you had an argument?' Devens continued with the questioning.

'Yeah. But it wasn't major… Just about moving out.'

'Would you expand?'

'Maddy wanted us to move into our own flat. I said I wasn't ready, and she got mad and said I was stalling. That I was choosing Moses over her. Anyway, it felt like an ultimatum, and I was pissed.'

'So, you left for work without resolving it?'

Jake nodded. 'Yeah. But I was going to talk to Moses. I just needed more time.'

'How would Moses have felt about you moving out?' Devens asked.

'He'd be sweet. He's a mate, and he'd understand. But I just wanted time to talk to him before I committed.'

'So, your fight wasn't about an affair?' Matthew asked, now sitting forward whilst Devens scribbled in his notebook.

'What?' Jake looked visibly stunned.

'Were you having an affair during your relationship with Maddy?'

'No!' he cried.

'Okay maybe *affair* is the wrong word. Were you sleeping with another woman?' Matthew asked.

Jake's silence was long, and Matthew pressed on.

'You see the thing is, Jake, we've spoken to Mrs Kirkoswald, or Esther to be more informal, and we understand that renovating her family home isn't the only thing you have been attending to?'

'Oh God!' Jake put his head in his hands.

'So let us ask you again. Were you sleeping around on Maddy? In particular, were you involved with Esther Kirkoswald? And more specifically, were you having sex with her on Friday 3 November, the date that Maddy disappeared?'

Nodding, Jake chewed his lip, anxiously looking around for an escape.

'Would you like to amend your statement?' Devens asked.

'Yeah,' Jake said, sounding defeated. 'I didn't go to the gym after work like I said. I stayed on at the site for a while.'

'Timings please, Jake?'

'Yeah, I got home after seven. Before that I was with Esther.'

The detectives continued questioning Jake, establishing that he had been sleeping with his client for the past six weeks and to his knowledge only his flatmate knew. Maddy didn't.

'So just to clarify. Your argument on Friday with Maddy wasn't about you sleeping around on her?'

'No! She didn't know. I wasn't going to continue it. I swear.'

Whilst they had successfully retrieved the new information, Jake continued to stick with his story that Moses came home around ten that night.

'I swear,' he said.

And Matthew almost believed him.

CHAPTER 48: ANNE-MARIE

By some careful planning, Anne-Marie had orchestrated an urgent client meeting in Perth, and within twenty-four hours, she was on a flight bound for Western Australia. She had justified it as "important" and "the only date possible" in her hastily typed email to her boss so desperate was she to see for herself if Henry was lying to her.

Anne-Marie didn't tell Nina or Louise what she was up to because she didn't want to be talked out of going. And there was a sense of self-preservation also taking place should her worst fears be realised.

The four-and-a-half-hour flight passed quickly as she availed herself of the movie channel and amenities of business class. Anne-Marie's corporate account with Qantas had earned her more than enough loyalty with the airline, and she was enjoying the continual food and beverage service from the attentive staff as the plane made its journey west. Well, there had to be some perks to working in the industry.

Anne-Marie was midway through her second film when the announcement came through that they would soon be descending into Perth. Reluctantly she unplugged her earphones and folded up her screen to prepare for landing and now had nothing to distract her from her nervous thoughts.

The sky was bathed in a delicious pink and orange sunset, and she focused on the city illuminated in pastels as they came into land.

An hour later Anne-Marie was standing at the check-in desk at the Langham Hotel, calmly handing over her credit card and smiling benignly. Instead of following her overnight bag to her suite, she made her way to the hotel bar for a glass of wine. Partly for Dutch courage and partly to reflect on what she was about to do.

She had Henry's home address in her phone, thanks to Matthew's detective work, and she was wrestling with whether to turn up unannounced or phone ahead. According to their brief text exchange, Henry had returned from Dubai. Assuming he wouldn't answer her call because he never did, her decision was made. Finishing her drink in one large gulp, she strode to the entrance of the hotel and was shown into a waiting taxi.

Twenty agonising minutes later she was at the address. Henry's home was everything she had expected. The lush bougainvillea hanging over the high white brick walls, which parted to show a winding, paved driveway leading up to a two-storey home. It was an enormous house with white shutters on the windows and a double dark timber front door. There were lights on inside the house, so she assumed that someone was home. But who?

Paying the driver, she got out of the taxi and walked timidly up the shadowy driveway. Her legs felt like jelly, and her heart thumped loudly in her chest. She kept to the side of gravel, hoping the head-high shrubs would keep her from being overly visible if someone was looking out of a window.

Was she really going to do this? Perhaps she should have gone with Matthew's suggestion of hiring a private detective to go in her place.

Suddenly she heard the purring of an engine noise and ducked behind one of the box hedges to avoid being exposed by the car's headlights.

Sure enough, a dark Maserati turned in to the property and roared up the driveway, stopping in front of the front doors.

She waited to see who stepped out of the vehicle and instantly recognised Henry, now illuminated by the sensor lighting.

He was every inch as handsome as his photos. His distinctive chiselled jaw and gloriously wavy brown hair catching in the light breeze. His slim-fitting suit hung off his athletic frame.

Dusting herself off, she was on the cusp of abandoning her hiding place but halted when the front door was flung open, the white light of indoors giving no mistake as to what she was seeing. A striking woman holding an infant on her hip.

She was beautiful. Her blond hair was swept up into a knot on her slender porcelain face, and her radiant smile landed on Henry. It was as if Anne-Marie were looking at Uma Thurman, the lithe beauty silhouetted in the massive door frame.

Like watching a car crash, Anne-Marie couldn't turn away and simply stared as her lover rushed to kiss the woman and child before the trio turned and walked inside, shutting the door behind them.

Anne-Marie felt sick. Bile rose up in her throat, and she felt physically winded at the disgustingly happy scene playing out in front of her. This was not a picture of an estranged husband and father. This was a couple in love. She had been cruelly misled. Henry had never mentioned having a small baby. How did she not know this?

In the minutes afterwards, Anne-Marie could only remain where she was, slumped behind the hedge.

She didn't know how long she sat there, but it was pitch-black when she eventually got up and tiptoed back to the roadway.

CHAPTER 49: LOUISE

It was Louise's third early start in a row, and the moaning that accompanied the six-o'clock alarm was getting shorter as the week progressed and her excitement intensified.

She had seen major progress already, the former dress shop transforming beautifully into a creative studio. Within ten days, the space would be ready for her to start her classes and host exhibitions.

She arrived just before seven and saw the tradie vehicles already parked waiting for her to let them in.

'Morning, Jonno,' Louise said, waving as she reversed her car in beside his.

'Hey, Louise, gorgeous day for it,' the builder replied. Jonno was overseeing the shopfront renovation and had been a godsend in coordinating the other trades, which included two carpenters, an electrician and plumber. A team of painters would start in earnest on Friday when the rest of the work had been completed.

Opening up the shop, Louise went up the street to fetch coffees, returning a short time later to distribute the drinks and confer with Jonno before leaving them to it.

Slipping into New Age Jewels was blissfully peaceful after the flurry of activity next door, and she moved into the back office to catch up on administration for a few hours before the time came to open up for the day.

She had hardly made a dent in the $100,000 business loan with the refurbishment costs coming in at less than $15,000, and that included the new furniture she had ordered.

Three whitewashed timber benches were due to arrive on Monday, along with fifteen matching stools. Louise had also ordered fifteen sets of tools for her aspiring jewellers, as well as branded aprons for them to keep as a memento of their class.

Right now she would focus on refining the schedule of children and adult jewellery classes, artists workshops and the evening masterclasses that would kick off only after she had ironed out any glitches.

She would need to employ another person, as between her and Jules they were already busy let alone running sessions next door.

Louise suddenly realised a way to keep her daughter close. Chloe would be just perfect!

CHAPTER 50: MATTHEW

Matthew and the team were sitting around the meeting table with morning coffees, listening to Moses and Jake.

The police device had picked up two conversations in the past twenty-four hours relating to the Madeline Bright investigation.

The first was on Monday night when Moses quizzed Jake about his visit to the Surry Hills Police HQ.

'So, what did the police ask?' Moses's voice crackled onto the digital recording, and there was a delay before Jake responded.

'I'm stuffed,' Jake groaned.

'What? What do you mean?' Panic radiated through the recording.

'They found out about Esther.'

'Shit! How come?'

'I don't know. They kept asking me about Maddy and why I hadn't been more concerned when I didn't hear from her on the weekend, and so one minute I'm fessing up that we had a fight and the next I'm fessing up to having an affair. Shit! I'm stuffed. They'll think it was me, won't they?' Jake's voice wobbled. 'How could they think I'd hurt Maddy? But shit, I bloody slept with

Esther and then had a fight with Maddy, so why wouldn't they be suspicious?'

'What did you and Maddy fight about?' Moses asked.

'Nothing, just leave it.'

The next night, another conversation materialised following the police's phone call to Moses. As planned, Davies had telephoned Moses to ask him to visit the police station on Wednesday morning to assist with enquiries, and it sparked Moses off again.

'Mate, I've now got to go in to see the coppers tomorrow,' Moses announced. 'What did you say to the police? Anything about me?'

'No,' Jake said, surprised. 'What do you mean?'

'Did you say anything about where I was? You know.'

'Nah. You mean on Friday? I don't even know where you went. All I said was that you and I watched basketball that night when you came in.'

'What time? What time did you say I came home?'

'Ten,' Jake answered.

'Sweet. Yeah, no worries.'

The following morning, Moses arrived punctually for his appointment, and the contrast between the two flatmates couldn't have been greater.

Jake had looked uncertain and anxious, whereas Moses oozed a confident bravado.

He was sitting tall and poised in the chair in the police interview room when Matthew and Devens walked in.

'Sorry to get you back in here,' began Devens as the two detectives sat down. 'Just keen to tie up a few loose ends, you know how it is.' His smile looked so genuine Moses relaxed back in his chair.

'No worries,' Moses said, taking a sip of the milky tea he had accepted earlier.

'We wanted to first see if you may have remembered anything about the last time you saw Madeline?'

'Nah, mate. Nothing.'

'No arguments or fights?' Devens persisted.

'Nah. All sweet.'

'According to your original statement, you slept in late on Friday 3 November and did not see Madeline that morning?'

'Yeah. Hungover, mate.' He gave a sly grin.

'But you got up to phone work at eight?' Matthew entered the interview, making an effort to look like he was reading from his file.

'Oh yeah.'

'But you didn't see Maddy when you made this call? Was she still in the flat?'

'Nah. Heard her leave.'

'Really? What time was that?' Matthew probed further. This was new information and something that Moses hadn't mentioned previously.

'Oh. Don't know. I was half-asleep, but I reckon around seven.'

'What makes you think it was seven?' Matthew kept at it.

'It could have been earlier. I didn't look at the phone, so I don't know. I went back to sleep, hey.'

'Yes, according to your original statement, you slept in until around two, and then you went for a surf first at Collaroy and then all the way up to Palm Beach where you then sat drinking a few beers and fell asleep before coming home around ten.'

'Yeah.'

'And according to your statement, you didn't meet up with anyone.'

'Nah.'

'So, there's no one to verify your movements?'

A glimmer of panic ran across Moses's smooth face but disappeared almost as quickly as it arrived.

'Would you agree to provide a DNA sample? Just to eliminate you from our enquiries, you understand?' Devens smiled politely at Moses, who looked like he was giving it serious thought before shaking his head.

'Nah, I'm all good.'

Matthew suggested a short break to refresh their beverages and brought Moses in another milky tea and black coffees for them.

'How well do you know Thredbo?' Matthew asked, trying for a new direction.

'Oh yeah. I've been there a few times.' Moses's answer sounded somewhat evasive.

'When were you there last?' Matthew asked.

'I don't know. Maybe September. Early.'

'Yeah?' Matthew probed, feigning being impressed.

'Yeah, I love snowboarding, you know.'

'We understand that you have a seasonal job at Thredbo and have for the past three years.' Matthew threw it out there and watched the colour drain from Moses's face.

Realising they knew more than he realised, he gave one of his sly grins. 'Yeah sure. I have a gig teaching sometimes. A mate of mine runs the ski school.'

'So, you've got a good knowledge of the mountain,' Matthew said.

'I s'pose.' Moses shrugged, remaining cool and elusive.

Little did he know that his used teacup was being sent to forensics for a sneaky DNA sample.

CHAPTER 51: NINA

Nina had made an extra fuss with her outfit, and even David had noticed, which was saying something given her husband's sole preoccupation with work of late.

'You're dressed up? Big meeting today?' David asked as she was fastening the zip on her new Armani dress in a soft blush pink.

She murmured her ascent, continuing to get ready.

Nina was having lunch with Sassy Swift and the Craylee executive, Dermott Sage, at the hottest new restaurant in Sydney to discuss a second contract with Sassy and the sparkling wine brand. Dermott had secured a table at the über fashionable French bistro Felippe, and Nina wanted to impress. The restaurant was near impossible to book, and she felt a frisson of excitement at what awaited her.

Nina couldn't deny her attraction for Dermott nor the connection she had felt with him in Tahiti. But, then again, a tropical paradise would make it difficult to resist anyone's charms. Especially given the strain between her and her husband of late.

Irrespective, it was nice to be appreciated by someone even though she had no intention of doing anything. She just wanted to feel good about herself for a few hours.

And Dermott didn't disappoint.

'You look beautiful,' he said, giving Nina a featherlight kiss to both cheeks before pulling out a chair at their table. The restaurant was intimate and buzzy and full. A cross section of businesspeople, entertainment figures and society women chatted noisily as a flurry of waiters criss-crossed the floor in haste.

'Would you like a glass of champagne?' Dermott asked as a waiter glided over to perform the duty of pouring her flute.

'Ahh, Bollinger, I see?' Nina smiled, noticing the vintage label on the bottle.

'Yes, I couldn't resist trying out the competition.' Dermott gave a self-deprecating laugh, and she found herself relaxing.

Dermott expanded on the meetings he had attended that morning, and Nina was interested in hearing about them. His work wasn't dissimilar to hers; they were both focused on finding the right strategic partners to work with. He too understood how fulfilling it was when likeminded partnerships were formed.

A loud ping erupted from Nina's mobile phone, which she had deliberately placed on the table in case Sassy needed directions to find them.

Nina, SO SORRY! Stuck in studio. Won't make lunch! x

'Oh, it's Sassy. The Mecca shoot has gone overtime, and she won't be able to join us.'

'No problem,' Dermott said easily. 'I'd still be happy to talk over what Craylee has in mind for the second campaign, and perhaps you could sound out Sassy when you next meet?'

Agreeing, Nina listened as Dermott outlined his thoughts whilst they shared mixed tapas plates and a bottle of chilled rosé.

'I'll send through a formal proposal,' he said, concluding the business talk as their table was cleared for their mains.

'So, onto other topics. How life's been since beautiful Tahiti?' he asked, refilling her glass. It had been a couple of weeks since their delightful escape, and memories of it brought a warm glow to Nina's face, which she found mirrored in Dermott's.

Why Anne-Marie wouldn't let her set up a drinks date with this gorgeous man, Nina would never understand. Dermott was perfect. But for whom, she now wasn't sure.

CHAPTER 52: ANNE-MARIE

Anne-Marie didn't know how she got through her morning appointments in Perth. One was a client meeting and the other an extended lunch, which was only bearable because she drank consistently through it.

'Shall I order another bottle?' asked Lucinda Waley, the marketing manager of a five-star hotel that Anne-Marie's firm wanted to do business with.

'Why not!' Anne-Marie was desperate to dull her emotions with copious wine.

'Wow. You're in good form, Anne-Marie,' Lucinda said, waving to a waiter to bring another bottle of the Shiraz they were drinking.

Anne-Marie had slept fitfully on the red-eye back to Sydney and called in sick when they landed. She was not only feeling dreadful from the alcohol she had funnelled into her system but strained from the emotional devastation of seeing with her own eyes what she had refused to believe.

Henry Dales was a lying, cheating scumbag.

And she had said as much in the half dozen text messages she had sent him when she had sat in the Qantas lounge, inebriated and feeling reckless.

The coward hadn't responded. And his profile on the online dating app had miraculously been deleted.

But who cared? She wasn't going to do anything scary. After all, she had wasted enough time on the illusion of Henry Dales.

It was time to *move on*.

But right now she needed to block everything out. She took two paracetamols, a sleeping table and went to bed.

Early the next morning, Anne-Marie struggled out of the sheets. She had contemplated going to the gym but couldn't find the motivation. What was the point? Who was she trying to impress?

Looking across at her phone, she realised she hadn't responded to Nina's text reminding her that the champagne executive was in town if she felt like meeting him for a drink on Wednesday.

No way, Nins, she thought, heading to the shower.

From now on, she would just be content without a man in her life.

They were far too much trouble in her opinion.

CHAPTER 53: MATTHEW

Matthew's blood was pumping when Moses casually strolled out of the police station. His cavalier attitude and smug confidence made Matthew even more determined to nail him.

When the interview had wrapped up, he had watched Moses lazily walk out to his ute and climb in. It was minutes later that Moses started up the engine and drove off, presumably to one of the addresses that had flashed up on his phone from WeWork Plumbing, his boss no doubt wondering where his tradesman was.

Matthew was now sitting around the conference table with Devens and the others.

'Let's work on pinpointing Moses's movements from the time Jake left the flat to Sunday morning when Madeline was discovered,' Devens was saying.

'Davies and Sorenson, go back and talk to neighbours. Find out if they remember seeing either man around the apartment block, drive off, return home. Anything.'

Because Moses and Jake parked their vehicles on the street, none of the neighbours in the apartment block could tell the uniform officer what time either had left for work or returned home.

'Ask again. Then go across the road, up the street, and talk to more neighbours. They are probably familiar with Jake's and Moses's trucks, but take pictures with you and question them about any sightings, usual or unusual.'

Devens also directed them to review any cameras on Barrenjoey Road to Palm Beach to check for Moses's ute on Friday afternoon and evening.

'We couldn't find his vehicle rego on the tollways for Friday or Saturday, so if Moses drove to Thredbo, he did it using an alternative route,' Davies said.

'Or he used another vehicle?' Matthew suggested.

'But the tyre treads at the scene are a close match to the ute he drives. He wouldn't switch up vehicles, especially if he was carrying a body, would he?' Sorenson asked. But Matthew was certain that Moses had driven to Thredbo and just needed a way to prove it.

'I'd like to examine Thredbo more closely. See if we can tie his DNA to the cigarette stubs. Learn more about Moses's knowledge of the mountain, that type of thing,' said Matthew, and Devens nodded, unaware of the detective's ulterior motive.

Thredbo. Snowboarding. Moses... Ella Williams? The sixteen-year-old snowboarder was still in the back of his mind. Could all the pieces fit in the same puzzle? He wondered.

CHAPTER 54: ANNE-MARIE
Friday 1 December

'Anne-Marie, can I see you?' her boss asked within minutes of Anne-Marie arriving at the office.

Anne-Marie quietly huffed, eyeing off the coffee and raisin toast she had been about to chomp into. Why couldn't she just be left alone to enjoy her breakfast before starting the workday? She was even ten minutes early!

Reluctantly pushing her toast aside, she picked up her coffee and followed Misha, begrudgingly sitting in one of the two visitor chairs opposite her desk.

It was only when Misha moved to shut the door behind them that Anne-Marie realised this wasn't a casual catch-up.

They generally got on well, enjoying an occasional wine after work and light banter around the office, but today's invitation didn't sound social. The closed door made her feel claustrophobic, and worry set in.

'You weren't well yesterday,' Misha began in a neutral tone.

'Sorry. I think I picked up a bug on the Perth trip,' Anne-Marie said, giving a weak smile.

'Yes, let's talk about the Perth trip. I've got the expenses here for the stay, and I'm having trouble reconciling the expenses to any client accounts.'

Anne-Marie felt lead in her stomach but pasted on a confident smile.

'It was a new business trip, Misha, so the expenses will all generate sales down the track. You know how it works?'

'Well, they will certainly need to, given the cost of the restaurant bill, the second bar bill, taxis and flights. Who signed off on this trip?' Misha pinned her with a stare.

Anne-Marie felt affronted. She had enough seniority by now to determine the validity of her business trips, and whilst the Perth trip had been construed to enable her to visit Henry, she had met two clients. Well, sort of clients. More suppliers if she was going to be honest with herself. But right now it was about saving herself from Misha's intense scrutiny.

'I didn't think I needed anyone to sign off, Misha. I've been working here for seven years now and never had a problem before with my work trips,' Anne-Marie said calmly, despite her annoyance at having to justify herself.

'But this really wasn't a valid work trip, Anne-Marie,' Misha admonished. 'You met with two existing contacts—who frankly should have been taking you out, not the other way around. Without a billable client over there that I can expense this to, I'm dumbfounded that you would fly over without consulting me first.'

Fury rose within Anne-Marie. She was being belittled by Misha, who she had always considered to be on her level but now was being brutally reminded was not. She was seething that she had to ask permission at this stage of her career to take a bloody work trip.

'If that's how you feel, then perhaps this isn't where I should be working,' Anne-Marie quipped.

'Taking unauthorised travel isn't on, Anne-Marie, and you know it,' Misha reprimanded.

'Just stick to your bloody unauthorised travel,' Anne-Marie snapped. 'I don't need to justify myself!'

'If that's what you want,' Misha said, looking slightly shocked at her outraged response. 'I will have HR draw up your termination settlement.'

'Fine,' Anne-Marie said, getting up from the seat and feeling rage sear through her.

Returning to her desk, she gathered up her handbag and jacket and was about to leave when she noticed the raisin toast sitting by her computer. Chucking the oily paper bag into the rubbish bin, she stormed towards the lift.

What had she just done?

CHAPTER 55: NINA

Meanwhile, Nina was back at the accountant's office that afternoon.

'It's not great news, I'm afraid,' began Miles Jeffries as they settled opposite each other at his large oak desk.

For the next fifteen minutes Nina listened as if in a daze...

'A discrepancy of $84,000 in the superannuation fund... a series of $6,000 loans monthly for the past five months from your personal chequing account... a second mortgage on your Bronte home...'

And this was all in addition to the financial woes she had only learnt about a few short days ago on her last visit to this office.

Nina's mind whirred with the effort of trying to calculate the shocking series of numbers, and then like a Band-Aid, Miles ripped it off in one fell swoop.

'We're looking at an amount of at least $788,000 plus the matter of the second mortgage,' he said, looking at her worriedly. Accountants were not meant to show this type of emotion. She needed him to pretend her situation was just a small blimp, something easily rectified. Revert to his gentle fatherly approach.

Miles continued, 'I'm really sorry, Nina. It's not good.'

His face conveyed sympathy but also, alarmingly, real concern. They had known each other a long time, before she had even set up her business, and now Miles was seeing her at possibly the worst time in her life.

'But how?' she stammered foolishly, already only too well aware of the answer.

'Your husband is a signatory to your personal and business accounts, which provides him with these funds at his disposal,' he said simply, shrugging.

Collapsing back into the seat, she deflated with a sigh and felt her stomach stir with nausea as white spots appeared before her.

'Are you okay?'

She shook her head slightly.

He got up and returned moments later with a glass of water. 'Take a mouthful,' he said, watching her cautiously. 'I'll fetch us tea with a hefty dose of sugar.' Miles disappeared to speak to his assistant, returning with two steaming mugs.

As instructed, Nina took tentative sips of the sweet liquid and no longer felt like she was going to pass out. Slowly her pulse calmed down and she felt more in control.

'Nina, there are avenues we can explore legally,' Miles soothed.

'You mean file charges against my husband,' she said despairingly.

How could she end up in such a pitiful position?

And why had David put her in it in the first place?

David had explained that his business had urgently needed a temporary financial boost when she had queried him about the initial credit card debt yet failed to disclose the full extent of his woeful financial position.

When she had pressed him about the other discrepancies—the withdrawals from her Reserve account and the bank loan on their Bronte home that week—he had become increasingly defensive.

'I know what I'm doing, just leave it to me. I'm sorting it out,' he had barked at her, walking out instead of staying to explain just how.

'Don't you have any faith in me?' was David's response when Nina had confronted him about the accounts again the next morning. 'I'm going to return the money soon. It's how finance works. Moving it around. You'll see. Have some faith.' He'd been almost flippant in her attempts for reassurance, making her feel foolish and distrusting for worrying about their mounting debts.

Today she was learning the true picture of what her husband had done, and it was overwhelming. David had been lying to her for months—if not years—and she was trying to grasp why.

CHAPTER 56: MATTHEW

Matthew should have been solely focused on the Maddy Bright case in front of him, but the Thredbo connection ate away at him. Could there be a link with the missing Ella Williams case?

Feeling compelled to learn more about Moses and his snowboarding link, Matthew looked up contact details for Mountain Ski Resort and began to dial.

The off season had hampered his efforts, and it was two days before Matthew had eventually tracked down someone from the company to speak to. The manager had confirmed that Moses Galvin was a seasonal employee of Mountain Ski Resort and had taught snowboarding at the mountain for the past five years.

'Yes, he'd know the back country well. All the instructors do,' the man had affirmed.

He didn't have too much more to offer, and so Matthew requested a list of students who had been booked into Moses's snowboarding sessions over the past two years. Matthew didn't mention this to Devens.

When the email arrived from Thredbo the following day, naming all the people who had received tuition on the slopes by Moses, Ella Williams's name was missing.

Dammit it! Matthew pounded his desk.

He was so sure she would be listed. But she wasn't. Ella Williams had not been registered for snowboarding lessons last year.

After scanning all the names on the list again, he shoved the printout into the Ella Williams file. And then a thought occurred to him. Why not go back two more years?

He returned to his laptop and began to reply to the resort manager to request the additional information, praying there would be something tangible to cling to. But right now he needed to return his focus to the case he was being paid to investigate and find further links that would connect his new number one suspect to the victim.

CHAPTER 57: NINA

Nina and Louise were sitting around the coffee table in Louise's lounge room that night. After the overwhelming meeting with her accountant, Nina couldn't face going home. She feared what she might say or do if she found David there.

Instead, she drove and drove, and before she knew it her car was pointed south heading to Canberra. Louise was her closest friend, so it wasn't a total surprise that she found herself turning to her in this time of crises. Despite the three-hour drive, she was in dire need of Louise's non-judgemental, unconditional support and reassurance that everything would be okay. And hopefully a dose of clarity too so she could figure out what to do about the strife she was in.

It was after eight when she arrived, and Theodore had given her a warm hug at the front door before disappearing into his study, leaving the women alone to talk.

'Come on, please eat a little more dinner otherwise Theodore will be insulted,' Louise fussed. As gourmet as the creation of lentils, pumpkin and ricotta lasagne was, Nina struggled to find her appetite.

'I could use more wine though,' she responded, twiddling the stem of her wineglass.

'Yes! Definitely more wine is in order!'

After splashing a generous refill in each glass, Louise resumed her spot back on the sofa.

'I'm worried about you girls,' Louise said, sympathetically watching Nina. 'Both of you. I'm pretty sure poor Anne-Marie has got herself caught up with either a scam artist or a married man with seven kids.'

'Yes, let's talk about Anne-Marie,' Nina said, relieved and desperate for a distraction.

Over the next hour they dissected Anne-Marie's online romance and their friend's blind spot when it came to Henry. The Perth businessman was perfect on paper, a handsome fifty-five-year-old mining executive, living in the salubrious suburb of Peppermint Grove, seeking an independent, outgoing woman to spend time with. But four months later, there had been very little time spent together. And zilch, if you took out phone calls and texts.

Sure, Perth was on the other side of the country, so it was a good four- or five-hours' flying time to be in the same city, but Henry had insisted that wouldn't be an issue for them when they first "met" online, claiming that he frequently visited the East Coast for business. However, those catch-ups hadn't materialised.

Henry had *apparently* tried to meet in Sydney a few times, according to Anne-Marie, who blamed herself for their inability to catch up on one occasion because she just was interstate at a travel conference. On another *supposed visit*, Henry's stay had been abruptly cut short, preventing any get-together.

'And don't forget all the plans that *conveniently* fell through,' Nina added. There had been at least three or four romantic weekends arranged—including the most recent birthday weekend in Sydney—but for one reason or another, Henry couldn't attend at the eleventh hour.

'It's just so hard seeing Anne-Marie putting on a brave face all the time,' Louise remarked.

'I know, but she won't listen to a word of criticism, which makes it hard to look out for her,' said Nina, who just wished Anne-Marie wasn't so proud that she couldn't admit when things weren't working. Anne-Marie had always had an idealistic image of how her life would be, and despite all the red flags along the way, she was persisting with this idealistic image of Henry.

'I offered to set up a drinks thing with Dermott—you know, the wine executive from Adelaide? He was in town this week, and I wanted to get her to meet him. But she refused, insisted that Henry was the man for her. I even texted her on Tuesday to see if she had changed her mind but didn't hear back.'

'I tried ringing her the other day. I think on Wednesday,' said Louise.

'How was she?' Nina asked.

'I don't know. She didn't call back either. Just a brief text to say she'd buzz soon. I hope she's okay.'

CHAPTER 58: LOUISE
Saturday 2 December

Louise was slathering butter on sourdough toast when Nina walked into the sunlit kitchen the next morning.

'Morning Lou, I always sleep so well here,' Nina sighed, giving her a squeeze.

Louise leant into the warmth of her friend's body, which felt too skinny yet more evidence of the toll her financial woes were having. 'I'm so pleased. I know you've had a few nights of no sleep at all.' She pressed the plate of toast into Nina's hands. 'Sit down, love, and I'll get you some spreads. And how about a coffee?' she asked, fussing around the kitchen. She had seen the dark shadows beneath Nina's anxious eyes when she had arrived exhausted yet manic the night before, and whilst the strain was still evident this morning, her friend appeared calmer, more restored.

Placing jars of jam, vegemite and peanut butter on the bench, Louise poured her a coffee. 'What's the plan for today?'

'Well, I don't think I can hide out here, as much as I'd love to,' Nina said, accepting the steaming mug.

'Of course you can. Stay as long as you like!'

'Thanks, Lou, but I need to get back and sort out next steps.'

'Do you want me to come back with you? Moral support and all that?'

Nina declined, reminding Louise that she had a shop to open this morning.

'I'm so proud of you, Lou! I can't believe the renovation is almost finished too,' Nina gushed.

'Yes, next Saturday I will be doing our first workshop! Woo hoo!'

CHAPTER 59: ANNE-MARIE
Tuesday 5 December

Anne-Marie had dodged Louise's and Nina's calls on the weekend and had only replied briefly to texts, claiming to be "flat out" and promising to "call soon". She had hardly left the flat in four days, not since her shock sacking on Friday.

She didn't know who she was angrier with. Henry for lying to her or Misha for humiliating her. She had really pulled the Boss card, making Anne-Marie feel like she was back at school and needed permission to leave the classroom.

What the fuck?

But most of all she was furious with herself.

Since storming out of the office, Anne-Marie had guzzled way too much wine and Netflix in her downward spiral. One minute she was fuming at the injustices she had endured, and the next, she was berating herself for her blind stupidity. The sexy lingerie she had bought for Henry was now in scraps in the kitchen bin, and all references to Henry had been deleted from her phone.

Another message buzzed through on the group message, this time from Louise, but as usual Anne-Marie ignored it. How could she admit to her closest friends that not only had she gone over to Perth to learn that Henry was a lying, cheating *married* bastard but that she had successfully lost her job? All within a week that she would rather forget. And she was doing her utmost to do just that, drowning her sorrows each night in bottles of pinot, greasy takeaway and sleeping tablets.

Anne-Marie contemplated getting off the sofa and having a shower but then thought better of it. *I'll just go back to sleep for a while.*

After all, there was nothing else to do...

CHAPTER 60: NINA
Thursday 7 December

Nina couldn't quite call it sleep as the night had been spent tossing and turning in a futile attempt to drift off. But eventually fatigue had won the battle and she had managed to doze for a few hours.

Now looking over at the empty side where David normally slept, she closed her eyes and silently willed herself not to cry.

They had had an almighty row on the weekend when she had confronted him about the disparities in their financial accounts from the missing funds from their self-managed superannuation fund to the mysterious monthly withdrawals from her personal account and the pièce de résistance, a second mortgage on their home!

'It's how the money game works, Nina,' David had quipped somewhat patronisingly, implying that it was she who was overreacting.

'David, we're talking about $800,000 of debits! Within six months!' she had screamed at him. 'How can you possibly spend that amount of money? *Our* money? And not talk to me first?'

'Oh, so you don't trust me?' David now shouted back.

'Where has it all gone?' Nina had dodged his question because she wasn't sure how she would answer.

'I told you, my business needed a leg up, that's all. It will all be repaid.'

'A leg up. That's what you said about the $22,000, which I might add you *again* took from my credit card without asking me. David, it's my business account not a joint account. How dare you just go helping yourself. What's going on with work? Are you in trouble?'

David began to lecture her like she was a student and not a very smart one at that. 'To make money you need to take risks, and they pay off in the long term. But in the short term, they don't. We're in the long game, and you just need to be patient.'

'So, what are we talking about here? How long is the long game?' she asked, desperate to understand.

'It could be six months. Tops. Maybe longer,' he said, shrugging his shoulders, and the evasiveness only served to irritate her further.

'Have faith in me, dammit,' he had repeated, but Nina's faith was diminishing fast.

'No!' she said suddenly, surprising herself. 'No more. You are not going to take another cent out of our accounts without joint signatories. And believe me, I won't be signing anything in a hurry.'

'You can't do that!' he bit back.

'I can. I'm authorising Miles and my solicitor to put an injunction on our accounts until we come to some workable plan.'

'How dare you! I need that money!' he spat, looking at her with contempt.

'David, we need to talk about this sensibly. Work out a plan. You can't keep propping up your business by putting us, my business, into debt.'

'You're so bloody risk averse, Nina.' He smirked. 'Always have been.'

'And you're incredibly irresponsible with money!' she snapped back.

'I don't need this.' He sulked, picking up his keys and slamming the front door.

That was last night.

Getting up, she padded downstairs to see if he had crept in late and slept on the sofa, but the house was empty in the early-morning light. His car was gone, and she knew he hadn't come back.

Perhaps today would knock some sense into him and they could work out a strategy to resolve their financial woes. A mess not of her making, but she felt compelled to find some solution because without one, where did that leave them and their marriage?

CHAPTER 61: MATTHEW
Friday 8 December

Matthew and the team had been at it all week, and progress was frustratingly slow.

Moses was their man, and they just needed the scientific evidence to back them up.

DNA would take at least another week if not longer in spite of Devens pulling favours with the lab.

So far, traffic cameras had yielded precisely nothing. No sightings of Moses's truck on Barrenjoey Road—which significantly diminished his claims to be surfing at Palm Beach. It was nearly impossible to access the peninsular without using that route.

Whilst that was good news, the bad news was that they couldn't find his vehicle on any of the cameras on the M1, M5 or M31 heading to Mount Kosciusko. If he had driven to Thredbo, his vehicle should have been captured.

Jake and Moses's neighbours remained mute on any sightings of the men in the apartment building or adjacent streets in the key twenty-four-to-forty-eight-hour period.

'But a woman in the top-floor unit of their Manly block said that she remembered there had been a tradesman visiting the building early that morning. She didn't mention it to the uniform police officer at the time because she didn't think it was relevant in the scheme of things. And because she didn't actually see the tradesman, just the vehicle.'

'Jesus!' said Devens, voicing what Matthew felt. Why were they only learning about this now? More than a month after the investigation had started.

'Yeah, I know,' sighed Davies. 'Anyway, the neighbour said that vehicle wasn't there for very long. She noticed it when she had returned from her morning walk around eight o'clock, and it was gone by the time she left to get her bus at nine-fifteen.'

'Any description of the vehicle? Or who the tradie was visiting?' Matthew asked.

'She didn't know which apartment they went to, and she was also pretty vague on whether the vehicle was a dual cab utility—like the type the boys drive—or an SUV. But she was certain that it was grey or silver.'

Great, thought Matthew, thinking of how many vehicles would fit into that extremely wide description.

'Okay, so she thinks it was a tradesman. Did she recall any markings on the vehicle—you know, a business logo name printed on the side?'

'No, just what I told you. She said she only noticed it because it was quite "large", and she had to walk past it to enter the building. The visitor spot is just outside the communal stairwell into the building.'

Devens ordered Davies to get the woman to visit the station and review a series of vehicle images to try to pinpoint more details on the make and model of the vehicle.

'Also, speak to all the neighbours—I don't care if it's by phone or face-to-face—and find out if anyone had a tradesman at their flat that day. And who.'

CHAPTER 62: LOUISE
Saturday 9 December

The refurbishments were completed, and the jewellery studio looked amazing.

The whitewashed furniture, neutral walls and large floor-length mirrors gave a sense of spaciousness and light. Louise felt butterflies in her stomach when she looked around at what she had created.

The sparkling rows upon rows of coloured and reflective beads and threads of silver and gold were the centrepiece of the room, and she felt the texture of the beads slip through her fingers. Her vision was now a reality.

In a few short hours Louise would be presenting the first workshop to her regular customers. Twelve of her most frequent shoppers—some had become good friends over the years—were arriving at ten for the inaugural class. To celebrate the launch, she was hosting the complimentary session and providing tea and coffee as well.

Louise had decided to road test the class with people who were supporters and familiar with New Age Jewels and also whom she knew would be constructive in their feedback. Plus it would be a chance to give back, rewarding them for their loyalty over the years.

Initially, just a couple of workshops would be presented, and then from late January, Louise would begin rolling out a more comprehensive schedule of guest artists, jewellers and metalworkers. She wanted to first experiment with how the classes would run before finessing things and bringing in guest instructors.

Chloe had eventually agreed to commit to a regular Saturday shift in the shop, which would provide a much-needed hand to Jules, her assistant. This way, Louise would be able to focus on managing the workshops. Her hope was that Chloe may one day take some of the classes, especially the ones catering for children, because her daughter had real talent and had learnt herself at such a young age.

Today's session would span two hours but would require at least four hours of Louise's time. An hour or so to set up everything and another hour at the end to tidy up and farewell her participants, who would hopefully be wearing big smiles and taking home a few purchases from New Age Jewels.

'Louise, what time is Chloe getting here?' Jules asked when Louise popped back into the shop after setting up for the workshop.

Louise looked at her watch and realised the first hour of store opening had flown by and Chloe hadn't yet arrived.

'I'll just text her now, Jules,' she said, adding another layer of anxiety to her already nerve-racking morning. In just one hour she would be presenting her first workshop!

But as the time arrived for Louise to slip next door and welcome her first jewellery students, there was still no sign of Chloe, and her texts had gone unanswered.

Louise had chipped her daughter a few times in the past about her tardiness and had reinforced the importance of being on time today but apparently to no avail.

'Sorry, Jules, I'll have to slip next door and start. Will you be okay here? I'm sure Chloe is on her way.' Louise gave a reassuring smile to Jules, who waved her off and wished her luck.

No doubt Chloe was running late (again), and Louise fired off a third text asking her to get to the shop ASAP.

There were twelve friendly faces sitting at the high benches ready for today's first session when Louise began to introduce the workshop theme, which was Festive Earrings, leveraging the Christmas season.

Here I go, she breathed and began.

CHAPTER 63: NINA

Nina was savouring a late-morning coffee on the deck, watching the active beach scene unfolding below. There was a shore break, emitting lots of shrieks, laughter and yelps as the swimmers attempted to remain upright and work their way out the back to the calmer waters. She hadn't managed to talk to David nor work out a solution for how to navigate the mess they were in. He was steadfastly avoiding her.

Since storming out of the apartment four days ago, Nina hadn't heard from him. There was evidence that he had been back to pick up clothes, but just where he was staying, she had no idea. And she didn't care. His passport was still in the safe, so that was something.

When Louise asked about David one night on the phone, she had broken down with the distress of it all.

'It's a nightmare, Lou. David's gone AWOL, refusing to discuss anything, let alone admit there's anything wrong.'

'You'll be fine. You've got your lawyer and accountant helping you, plus you've got us.'

'But what if I lose my business? I'm pretending everything is fine at work, but it must be bloody obvious how much stress I'm under. I'm out of the office more and more either at legal meetings or seeing Miles.'

'You're always dashing in and out to see clients; believe me they wouldn't have noticed,' Lou soothed.

Not long after ending their call, Nina heard a buzz and went to answer it.

'Hey stranger,' said Anne-Marie meekly.

'Oh, Anne-Marie, it's so good to see you!'

'I'm sorry I've been away with the fairies. I spoke to Lou, and I know things aren't easy for you right now. I hope you don't mind me just turning up?'

'It's a mess—' Nina's voice caught, and Anne-Marie pulled her into a hug.

'It will be okay, Nins,' Anne-Marie whispered into her ear.

Later, over strong coffee, Nina detailed the extent of the financial crisis she was in and her absent husband. She feared losing both her home and possibly her agency if the debts were recalled.

As Nina offloaded her fears, she found a new resolve. She had been so blind about her business and personal affairs, meekly hoping for David to fix things. But now she felt a decision had been made.

Enough! It's game on, David. I'll see you in court! Yep, that's exactly how much I trust you!

CHAPTER 64: LOUISE

'Welcome, ladies, and thank you for coming to my first jewellery-making workshop,' Louise said, delighted to see the encouraging smiles and excited faces reflected back at her.

Louise spoke animatedly about the festive holiday theme of the class, which would see each person leave with a bespoke pair of earrings to wow family and friends this Christmas or to a New Year's Eve soirée. She outlined the tools in front of them and how they would be used in each of the steps to assembling their earrings. And then she dazzled them with the showcase of colourful beads and metal wires they could choose from.

For the next hour and a half, Louise roamed around the room, spending time with each person and guiding them through the process of their jewellery creation. The energy in the room was electric.

As the workshop drew to a close, Louise encouraged everyone to wear their creations and stay on for a cup of tea or coffee and Christmas shortbread. Later, as she packed up the tools and beads, she watched as more than a few made their way next door to browse at New Age Jewels, making her smile.

When Louise walked into the shop a little later, she saw a few of her workshop participants scouring the designs and Jules assisting another customer in her usual easy manner. Louise settled herself behind the cash register to attend to a waiting customer and then went to serve a few women who were anxious for her advice.

It was sometime later that Louise asked Jules about Chloe. She had simply assumed her daughter had been on a lunch break, but it had now been at least an hour since Louise had returned from the workshop.

'What time did Chloe go to lunch?' Louise asked Jules, looking at her watch.

'Chloe? She hasn't been in,' Jules replied puzzled. 'I thought she must have texted you?'

'What? You mean she didn't arrive earlier?'

But Jules just shook her head.

'Okay, you better take a break, Jules, and I'll keep an eye on things here.'

'Shall I get you your regular toastie?' Jules asked, and Louise could have hugged her for her thoughtfulness.

When the front door had closed, Louise had the shop to herself and quickly rang her daughter. How could Chloe let her down on such an important day?

Louise's call went to Chloe's voicemail, again, and in minutes the door was sounding with a new customer and Louise got on with the afternoon trade.

By the end of the day, Louise was exhausted but not too tired to make the drive to Chloe's house in Dixon on her way home. Enough was enough. Today was a big deal for Louise and her new venture, and Chloe knew that. Louise felt a powerful wave of disappointment in her daughter.

Knocking on Chloe's front door, Louise noticed the shared house was looking especially unkempt with an unruly front garden and mail spilling out of the wonky letterbox. She couldn't remember the last time she had visited and made a mental note to organise a gardener to come over and sort out the overgrown lawn and bushes.

A young woman opened the door, but it wasn't Chloe's flatmate Emily.

'Hi. I'm Louise. Chloe's mum. Is she here?'

'She's sleeping,' said the woman, who looked like she had been woken by Louise's knock.

'I'm Shelby, come in.' She gave a shy smile, leading Louise inside and disappearing into one of the bedrooms.

Tapping on Chloe's door, Louise gently pried it open to see the room was dimly lit by the last rays of the day's sunshine slipping through the sides of the ill-fitting curtains.

Louise could see a lump of duvet tangled in the middle of Chloe's queen-size bed and walked over to pull the curtains open to let in some much-needed light.

As she turned towards the bed, she expected to hear her daughter's groans, but instead the room remained silent. Sitting down on the mattress, Louise tentatively pulled back the cover.

'Chloe?'

No response.

Touching Chloe's face, her skin felt cold and clammy.

'Chloe? Wake up, sweetheart.' Louise gently shook her daughter to raise her out of her slumber, but she was dead to the world.

Looking across at her bedside table, she gasped in horror.

A small glass pipe was sitting there, dirty and discarded. Beside it a lighter and empty foil wrap. 'Oh my God!' Louise knelt over Chloe, now shaking her more vigorously into consciousness.

'Whaaa?' Chloe mumbled.

'Chloe. Wake up!' Louise urged, her heartbeat now a frenzy.

But she failed to generate any more response from her drowsy daughter. Quickly she went to get her mobile phone out of her handbag and dialled triple zero.

'Come on, Chloe, come on. Wake up. Please,' she sobbed as she waited for the ambulance.

****

'Your daughter has suffered from an overdose, and we have administered Narcan to reverse the effects of the opioid in her system,' said an emergency doctor, who looked not much older than her eighteen-year-old daughter.

'It was a good thing you brought her in so quickly. Heroin overdoses are notoriously fatal—'

'Heroin?' Louise yelped. 'No, no. No! God no! Chloe wouldn't take heroin. She wouldn't even know what it was.'

'Hey, Louise, it's okay. Let the doctor finish.' Theodore put a hand on her shoulder, and she felt calmed by his quiet presence.

'I'm sorry to say that Chloe has suffered the effects of an overdose of heroin. Toxicology will confirm this, but from the way she presented to emergency—her pinned pupils, irregular heartbeat and slow breathing and her unconsciousness—there can be little doubt. You recall the pipe you found?'

'Yes,' Louise said weakly. 'I gave it to the nurse earlier.'

'It was found to have traces of the drug. I'm sorry,' he said, looking at Louise and Theodore, and she wondered how someone so young could be the one reassuring the parents of a child.

Theodore took over the conversation as Louise moved over to Chloe's beside and slumped into the chair beside her.

She looked so peaceful in her sleep. So innocent. But now Louise knew that her little girl's innocence was no more.

CHAPTER 65: MATTHEW

Matthew arrived at the swanky inner-city bar first. It was a much more sophisticated establishment than Stevo's, the only other watering hole he had frequented since arriving in Sydney a month ago. The moody elegance around him was in stark contrast to the dark, raucous pub, and he wasn't sure which one he preferred.

As he ordered a craft beer, he looked around the polished crowd of young people enjoying a Saturday night. Their voices were muted and the music low.

Paying for his beer, he found a high table with two bar stools and sat down to observe the well-heeled Sydney crowd at play.

He was only a few mouthfuls in when Anne-Marie arrived, looking just as glamorous as the others in the bar, but flustered. Her silky white jacket and slim-fitting black pants accentuated her curves, and the high ponytail she wore added a girlish note, softening her usually steely impression.

'Sorry.' She grimaced.

'No worries,' he said, standing up. 'Let me get you a drink?'

'Oh thanks. A pinot or Shiraz would be great.'

Returning a few minutes later, Anne-Marie appeared more composed, her jacket now shrugged off and hanging on the back of her chair and her tanned, toned arms relaxed on the table.

'How's the case going?' she asked, taking a sip of her wine.

'Okay. A slight hold-up right now, but hopefully next week will be more rewarding.' The past week had been agonisingly unproductive in terms of discovery, and Matthew was relieved to have plans this evening. Even if they weren't purely social.

'Cheers,' he said, lifting his glass to hers before taking a mouthful. 'How have you been?' he asked. Anne-Marie had requested they meet, and he was curious.

'Fine,' she breathed out before taking another sip and beginning to squirm in her seat. He waited patiently, and she realised the carefree act was useless.

'Well, no, not fine.' She put her glass down and began fidgeting with the coaster. 'You were right about Henry.'

'You asked him?'

'No. Worse. I went over there and saw him.' She sighed.

'Anne-Marie, I could have got my contact over there to get you the proof.'

Anne-Marie just shook her head. 'I don't think I would have believed them.'

He listened to her story of huddling behind the bushes in Henry's driveway, watching the scene of a happy family play out.

'I'm so humiliated and embarrassed. I don't know really what's worse. Falling for the age-old lie or refusing to heed anyone's warnings, including yours.'

She looked down at the now shredded pile of cardboard, the remnants of the coaster that she had taken out her anger on.

She was engulfed in grief and despair, and he reached over to hold her trembling fingers.

'It will be okay, Anne-Marie.'

She silently nodded, and he let her hand go, reaching into his jacket for his phone and notebook.

'How can I help?'

'Promise me this will just stay between us? Louise won't know?'

Matthew nodded.

'I've done something stupid. I sent explicit photos of myself to him, and I'm worried that he might do something with them. You know, upload them? Or share them with friends?'

Matthew was surprised that this tough-talking brunette would make herself so vulnerable.

'Could you like warn him off or something? Get the images destroyed? I don't know, just put the fear of God into him?' she pleaded.

The tan had now drained from her face, and her desperate eyes searched his.

'Sure. I can give him a call and remind him of the possible charges for using a carriage service to transmit private images, that sort of thing,' he said, understanding how a police phone call may help her situation but keener to placate her.

'Thank you,' she breathed out.

'Hey, why don't I get another round of drinks?' he suggested. He didn't want her going home in this rattled state. Plus there was still so much he didn't know about Anne-Marie.

She gave a small nod and wiped her eyes. 'I'll just go find the Ladies and freshen up. I'm sure I look like a wreck.'

Watching her leave to find the restrooms he thought, *No you don't. You actually look adorable and approachable for the first time.*

CHAPTER 66: ANNE-MARIE
Sunday 10 December

Anne-Marie rolled over in bed to glance at the digital clock. She would need to get up shortly to meet her cycling mates at Centennial Park, but she still had a few minutes to just lie and return to the events of last night.

She had been pleasantly surprised by Louise's friend Matthew. He had been unexpectedly kind to her. Instead of berating her for her stupidity or lecturing her about Internet Fraud 101, he had been the opposite, showing a sensitivity and compassion that she didn't feel she deserved.

God, I'm such an idiot! she silently cursed herself for the hundredth time, curling into a foetal position.

Yet when she had said something similar last night, Matthew had gently reassured her that modern internet dating was very clever at drawing in smart women, just like her.

He had made her feel less of a fool, and that was really nice of him. Something he didn't have to do.

God knows where her embarrassing photos were going to end up, but Matthew had committed to warning Henry of the perils of doing anything stupid with him. She just hoped Henry had deleted them now, like she had wiped his.

Sighing, Anne-Marie pulled off the bed sheet and moved to find her Lycra gear.

Today would be the start of a new era; she felt it in her bones.

CHAPTER 67: LOUISE

A day after the shocking discovery of her comatose daughter, Louise arrived home with Chloe. She had insisted that Chloe stay with them, and her daughter didn't have the energy to argue.

Chloe was pale and fragile as she moved tentatively to sit on the sofa.

The doctor had explained that in the next twenty-four hours, Chloe's body would continue to show symptoms of withdrawing from the drug, and Chloe was already feeling dreadful. She was fatigued and had vomited several times. She would also experience aches and pains and agitation to set in.

When Chloe refused anything to eat, Louise returned with two cups of English Breakfast tea.

'Thanks, Mum.' Chloe looked shamefaced as she sat cross-legged on the lounge, her large sweater engulfing her lean frame. Her gaze lowered.

Refusing to cry, Louise just nodded and took a sip. She hadn't pressured Chloe for an explanation when she had sat beside her bed in the hospital, but now that they were home, she needed to know.

'Why, Chloe?' she pleaded.

Watching tears fall down her daughter's face, Louise's heart gave a tug, and she felt her eyes water in sympathy. Reaching for a tissue in her pocket, she wiped her face.

'I just want to understand?' Louise said, willing her daughter to explain.

'You can't, Mum.' Chloe sniffled.

'Please let me try?'

But Chloe just shook her head.

'We were so worried, Chloe.' Louise's voice cracked, and she had to use every ounce of energy to hold it together.

'Your father and I love you so, so much. And we couldn't bear to see something terrible happen to you. Ever again,' Louise said calmly, willing herself not to tear up again. 'You are our pride and joy. We don't want to lose you.'

'You're not going to lose me, Mum,' Chloe whispered, giving Louise a watery smile.

'But we nearly did.' Louise sniffled.

'I didn't mean to overdose. I must have smoked too much,' Chloe said. 'I'm so sorry, Mum.'

'Oh darling, I just want to understand why you would want to take drugs?'

'Everyone does,' she murmured. 'I was just experimenting. That's all it was.'

'Chloe, you ended up in ICU,' Louise said, more sternly than she intended. 'You nearly died!'

Chloe put a hand to her eyes and wiped the blobs of tears streaming down her face and spilling onto her pale sweater.

'Will you promise me you won't do it again,' Louise begged.

Wiping her face with her sleeve, Chloe sniffed and nodded. 'Don't worry, Mum. I never want to do heroin again.'

****

'I just think we need to get professional help,' Louise said to Theodore later that night as they were curled up in the lounge room, their daughter sleeping peacefully upstairs.

'But didn't she say she wasn't going to do drugs?'

'Well, she said she wouldn't do heroin again. Look, I know drugs are part of the youth culture, but if she goes down that road, I just worry she might not make it out again. She doesn't have the structure of school anymore and hasn't even confirmed if she's going to go to university next year.'

Louise recalled her own wild youth, and if Chloe had inherited her risk appetite and was dabbling in class A drugs, the consequences were frightening. Louise had mucked around with drugs when she was her daughter's age, especially when she was dating Rex and part of the whole rock 'n' roll scene. But nothing in the league of heroin.

Over the past few days, Louise had done extensive reading and was staggered to learn that one in four people who try heroin become addicted. She was also astonished that heroin was in fact relatively cheap to source—as little as thirty dollars for a hit. A nasty habit could end up costing around $150 a week and take a lifetime to quit.

One article she read said that people who smoked heroin were often new to drug use and scared to inject, which was mildly reassuring. Surely that was Chloe? Although, the article went on to say that most users eventually wound up injecting, due to the highly addictive nature of the drug.

'Heroin frightens me! It's not a party drug like ecstasy or marijuana. Not that I want Chloe taking those either,' Louise stipulated, knowing she was being a little hypocritical, but this was her daughter's life she was protecting. 'From what I've read, heroin is about extreme pleasure, it affects the brain's response and delivers powerful feelings of relaxation, pleasure and bliss. It makes me worry that Chloe is trying to escape from something—even if it's just the day-to-day grind.'

Theodore squeezed her hand. 'Darling. I'll support you if you want us to get help, but I truly feel that Chloe was just experimenting. Let's not forget the wildflower I met all those years ago?'

She hugged her husband. He had been her rock since those tumultuous days of excesses. Excessive emotions with her boyfriend at the time, excessive partying and late nights, and basically being excessively irresponsible.

Thank God Theodore had come into her life when he did. But then again, she was also at a time when she wanted to change her ways. Settle down, have her own family. She knew Chloe would need to want to get on the straight and narrow. That was when the battle would be won.

CHAPTER 68: NINA

Nina was floating out of her early-morning yoga class at her local yoga studio and contemplating picking up a coffee before heading home to shower and leave for work when her mobile rang.

It was her accountant.

'This is early, Miles,' she said breezily, still enjoying the lofty effects of her Yin class.

'I'm sorry to call first up in the morning,' he apologised. 'I just thought you would want to know.'

Nina felt suddenly very alert and stopped walking.

'David is being investigated by ASIC for trading whilst insolvent. Essentially, it prevents him from trading for now, but it may also have implications for you. I'm sorry, Nina. It's not good.'

Nina let out a huge sigh. It was obvious David had been sailing close to the wind with his business, constantly moving money around to keep things afloat, including money from her business accounts, but she didn't consider that it would come to this.

Agreeing to meet Miles at his office at nine, Nina went home to shower and rearrange her morning's schedule of meetings. This couldn't wait.

A short time later she was sitting opposite Miles in his office, which she was becoming all too familiar with and not for the right reasons. Even her preferred beverage, a green tea, was waiting for her.

'What I have been able to learn is that there has been an investigation by the Australian Taxation Office as well as the Australian Securities and Investment Commission into past annual financial statements for your husband's financial planning business.'

'But why? Who notified them?'

'There's been a crackdown generally in the financial advisory space, so it might have been because the ATO and ASIC are taking a greater review of all firms. Or it might have been a whistle-blower within the firm, or even a disgruntled client.'

'Do you think David will think the whistle-blower was me?'

'There's nothing to indicate that nor has any such implication been made. Anyway, that's the least of our worries.' Miles opened a folder and flicked through to locate a sheet outlining Nina's property and financial assets.

'In times of proven insolvency, the penalties are fierce for directors. Fines, compensation and even imprisonment. What the authorities are seeking to find out is whether David was trading without having the financial means to pay his debts. In some cases, civil charges are also imposed, such as when a director provides misleading financial reporting, including signing a director's declaration about the solvency of the business, the accuracy of its financial reports, that type of thing.'

Nina could see that Miles had highlighted a number of items on the document with a red pen.

'These assets here, Nina, the ones I've noted, are assets that are in your joint names, and they will be liable to cover the debts of David's company.'

Nina could see them clearly, but Miles pushed the document closer towards her.

Her house. The beautiful Bronte apartment that she had spent months and months redesigning and transforming into her sanctuary was one of the items in red.

'Essentially the creditors are the first ones looked after in situations like these, and the number one creditor will be the Tax Office and then the banks that hold the loans.'

David owed millions according to the intelligence that Miles had been able to gather.

With shaking legs, Nina left the accountant's office and began to make her way back to Talent Time.

The notion of losing her home to pay David's debts was all too terrifying.

CHAPTER 69: MATTHEW
Tuesday 12 December

'Bingo!' Matthew punched the air, putting his mobile back on the desk.

'Who was that?' Davies asked.

'Constable Jenny Dillon from Jindabyne. On Friday 3 November at 2:13 p.m., an SUV registered to a Delia Evans was clocked driving into Mount Kosciusko National Park and then exiting the park at 3:58 p.m.'

Matthew now had Sorenson's and Davies's attention, both scrutinising what was coming.

'This is where it gets interesting. First, Delia Evans—who lives in Cooma and has an annual Park pass—claims she was overseas at the time.'

The questioning faces of his colleagues were priceless.

'*And...* Delia Evans just happens to be the mother of a certain person of interest.'

'Moses Galvin's mother?' Sorenson's eyes were like saucers, her disbelief mirroring his own.

'Yep. One and the same.'

'My God!' Sorenson shrilled.

'Bloody brilliant!' Davies thumped his desk several times, prompting Devens to raise an eyebrow when he entered the department.

Matthew had enlisted the National Parks and Wildlife parks head ranger Guy Swan to provide a full list of all vehicle registrations photographed entering and exiting Mount Kosciusko National Park on Friday 3 November. Unlike the first time around, the police didn't rule out locally registered vehicles or park employees, nor were they only focused on registrations connected to the three males of interest to their investigation: Jake Smith, Moses Galvin and the schoolteacher, Clayton Jones.

There were 427 vehicles in total that entered and exited the park that day, and his Jindabyne colleague had done the painstaking work of telephoning each vehicle owner to confirm their visit and establish any connection to the current investigation.

On Constable Jenny Dillon's three hundred and third call, she had hit gold.

'We believe Moses used his mother's vehicle to drive in and out of Kosciusko,' Matthew explained.

The vehicle registration details and photo imagery captured at the entry gates would be emailed through within the hour, and Matthew strongly suspected the person driving the vehicle would be Moses. It certainly couldn't be his mother.

This could be the breakthrough Matthew needed.

'I'll call the Cooma guys and get them to impound the vehicle,' he said, and Devens nodded as he digested the update.

The SUV would be taken into the police yard for testing of tyre treads and any DNA matches to Moses and Maddy.

The next forty-eight hours were the longest of Matthew's life.

The photographic image of the SUV entering Kosciusko National Park was grainy, and whilst it showed the vehicle, the driver was less discernible. The tech guys would spend time cleaning it up and seeing if they could find Moses's face in there somewhere. It didn't look likely, given the poor quality of the image, but they would try.

The SUV had been towed into the police yard, and a forensic team, including Reynor, were now in Cooma poring over it. The Toyota Rav4 SUV was gunmetal grey.

Cooma Police interviewed Moses's mother, Delia Evans, and were now relaying the contents of the interview to Matthew and Devens.

'Mrs Evans said that she was holidaying in Bali for three weeks with a girlfriend. They left October twenty-seventh and returned November seventeenth,' said Sergeant Mike Stewart.

They could easily check it out, but Matthew couldn't see why she would lie about something that was so easy to confirm with authorities.

'According to Mrs Evans, the SUV was in Sydney whilst she was overseas, so she doesn't know why it would be on the Mount Kosciusko camera on the third unless one of the boys borrowed it,' the officer said.

Matthew and Devens exchanged a look as they continued listening to the sergeant over the speakerphone in Devens's office. In addition to Moses, Delia Evans had an eighteen-year-old son from a second marriage. Teddy was in his final year at school and living with his father in Blacktown.

'Mrs Evans said that neither son had mentioned visiting Cooma, or Mount Kosciusko for that matter, nor using her vehicle whilst she was away, but she hadn't caught up with them since getting home from her trip. She's confirmed they both have front door keys and can come and go as they want.'

'Where did she leave the car? In Sydney?' Matthew asked.

'She said that she parked it on a side street in Balgowlah, near Moses's flat so that he could keep an eye on it. He then dropped her and her friend at the Manly wharf so they could get the ferry to Circular Quay and the Airport Train to the international terminal for their evening flight.'

After extracting the specific location details for the SUV, Matthew organised for a Manly police officer to visit the neighbourhood and find out if anyone saw the vehicle and also if someone matching Moses's description was seen driving the vehicle on Friday 3 November or Saturday 4 November.

Hopefully neighbourhood watch was alive and well in the northern beaches and they could begin to plot the man's journey south.

But first he wanted to start at the source. 'Davies, can you also get back in touch with the resident from unit nine and show her the image when we get it? See if it's the same vehicle she remembered seeing in the visitor spot last month? So far, she's the only one in the building who recalls noticing it parked there.'

MICHELLE LARMER

CHAPTER 70: LOUISE

Louise and Theodore juggled taking turns to be at home with Chloe, too anxious to leave her on her own.

Theodore worked from his study, and Louise scheduled Jules on for a few extra shifts in the shop.

Louise had immediately postponed the two jewellery workshops she had scheduled for this weekend and was contemplating cancelling her pre-Christmas one too. But the class had been fully booked as soon as she had announced it on her Facebook page, and she didn't want to let anyone down this close to Christmas. She knew some of those coming were planning to create gifts, plus Anne-Marie was going to be there to work in the shop and help out. Louise hadn't asked Anne-Marie how she had managed to get the week off work so easily, but there would be time enough to hear all about that.

For now, she would use this week to take Chloe to her appointments with the psychologist that had been recommended by the hospital.

'I don't need a shrink!' Chloe had protested when Louise had taken her to her first session.

'God, Mum, everyone is making too big a deal of this!' Chloe had stomped up the stairs to her bedroom and hurled her small body onto the bed, face down. 'Arggh!'

Louise followed her into her bedroom and sat down beside her.

'Chloe, you almost died,' Louise said quietly, baffled that her daughter didn't comprehend the grave situation that greeted them all just a week before.

'Mum, it wasn't that bad. And I wasn't trying to kill myself, despite what everyone is thinking,' Chloe mumbled, turning her body to face her mother.

Sighing, Louise leant over to hold Chloe's hand. Whilst Chloe didn't return the grip, Louise persisted with a few light squeezes.

'It was, darling. I was there. You weren't conscious, and it was touch-and-go there for a while. I don't want to scare you, but you need to know how serious it was in that hospital room. All we want is for you to have professional help. Someone who is trained to know how to guide you through this and who knows what you might need. Even if it's just an objective listener.'

'But it was just for fun, Mum. I'm not a head case.'

'Heroin is not for fun! It's an opioid that affects your developing brain. And it's highly addictive. I know you might be playing around with other drugs too.' Louise and Theodore had been informed of the toxicology report on their daughter and her excessive alcohol and drug use.

'This is incredibly serious, and that's why your father and I are getting the best help available at the Huntington Retreat, the one that Eleanor recommended,' Louise continued, reminding her daughter that on the advice of her psychologist, a two-week stay at a full-service facility was the best way to help her break her worry habit of dabbling with drugs to lift her mood or deliver oblivion.

Sniffling, Chloe sat up and squeezed her mother's hand.

'We just want to understand why? Is taking drugs really just for fun? Or are you using them for something else?'

Louise had wondered if her daughter was just simply idle and restless or was there a bigger issue at hand. Was she self-medicating to seek an escape route from something painful in her life?

'Please just go to these appointments and Huntington next week, for me and your dad?' Louise felt reassured by another slight squeeze from Chloe's pale hand.

Louise wanted to broach Chloe's plans for next year and insist that she commit to either university or embarking on something constructive and concrete. Her gap year hadn't delivered the happy, carefree life they were expecting, instead Chloe had slept through half of it and worked in dive bars and partied for the other half. It seemed the crowd she'd been partying with were a wild and scary lot, and she didn't want Chloe's reckless lifestyle to continue. And it wouldn't, if Louise and Theodore had any say in it.

But for now, Chloe had agreed to undergo the counselling and rehabilitation retreat, and that would be enough. Theodore had given notice on her room at the share house and paid two months' rent so that her flatmates wouldn't be left in the lurch.

CHAPTER 71: ANNE-MARIE
Wednesday 13 December

Anne-Marie had been scouring the job listings on LinkedIn, Seek.com.au and EverTravel, a specialist site for the travel industry. The lack of anything remotely similar to what she had been doing was depressing.

It was like her years of experience in corporate travel were about to be reduced to a dumbed-down version, and she would be catering for customers who wanted to spend the least amount of money in the cheapest country and with the least cultural experience possible. A tacky resort at Phuket or the cheapest seats to Europe would be the requests coming her way. She was on the verge of giving up her search and even contemplating crawling back to her mean boss, but just then a job advertisement caught her eye.

PRIVATE TRAVEL AND LIFESTYLE MANAGER

"An experienced professional specialising in the fields of travel and executive assistance is sought by a private business to commence immediately. Your role would be to coordinate all travel requirements for an executive client and manage a highly complex diary and schedule. Must be highly organised, efficient and discreet. Apply…"

Anne-Marie was intrigued with the role, which would be far removed from the grind of working away in a travel agency. She was curious to know more about the "executive client", but there wasn't anything that revealed who they were or the type of business they represented.

She even telephoned the recruitment company listed with the classified only to be politely directed to "please apply if you wish to be considered", and so she duly did.

After pressing Send on her cover letter and résumé, her phone lit up with a message from Matthew.

Good to see you the other night. Swamped on a case right now, but I haven't forgotten about your request. Update soon. M

Quickly tapping a thanks, she then picked up her phone to call Louise. She wanted to squeeze more information out about this surprising detective. Not that she was interested or anything, but just because… Well, he was different to what she had initially expected.

'Anne-Marie? Hi…' Louise's voice sounded wary. As if she was caught mid-customer.

'Sorry, love, have I got you in the shop?'

'No, no. I'm at home,' Louise said, clearing her throat.

'Is everything okay?'

'Fine.'

In all her time of knowing Louise, "Fine" wasn't a word she used. Lou was chilled, creative, happy… but never "fine".

'What's happening?' Anne-Marie probed cautiously.

'What do you mean?'

'Lou. It's me you're talking to,' Anne-Marie said, pausing for her friend to spill.

And spill she did.

Chloe.

Heroin overdose.

Counselling.

Rehab.

'My God, why didn't you let us know?' Anne-Marie wailed, knowing she hadn't been the most communicative of late herself.

'Chloe is really upset—as are we. We're just getting things sorted out, and to be honest, I didn't know how to say hey, my beautiful, angelic daughter is in hospital with a drug overdose,' Lou said, before bursting into tears.

'What can I do?' Anne-Marie pleaded after hearing Lou's sobs.

'Nothing love… We're taking Chloe into a rehab facility on Sunday morning, and she will stay there for two weeks. Maybe we can catch up next week whilst I'm trying to distract myself from it all.'

Anne-Marie calculated the dates and worked out that Chloe would be in treatment over Christmas.

'I know.' Louise sniffled. 'But her health is our major priority right now.'

'Well, you know what, why don't I come down on Sunday night and stay on to help out with the shop next week? I can even stay over Christmas and get some festive cheer going? I promise to be in charge of decorations, cooking, cleaning. You can just focus on Chloe and selling bling to Christmas shoppers.'

'Oh, that would be so lovely. We haven't even got our heads around Christmas this year. A slight distraction—first with the shop refurb, then of course everything with Chloe.' The relief in Louise's voice was heartbreaking.

Anne-Marie hung up the phone a short time later, feeling that she had real purpose. She had offered to help out in Lou's shop next week, stepping in for Chloe, who she knew Lou had been counting on in the busy Christmas shopping week. Plus it wasn't like Anne-Marie had a job of her own to go to. She hadn't mentioned this to Lou, but she would when her friend was in a better frame of mind. She had enough worries in her world right now.

CHAPTER 72: NINA

'Sassy Swift is waiting in the conference room,' said Lee Lamone, stopping by Nina's office.

Nina had completely zoned out for God knows how long and wasn't feeling at all ready to meet the agency's number one star.

'Right!' Nina mustered a bright smile, watching Lee scrutinise her cautiously from the safety of the door frame. 'I'll see you in there. I just need to get the lippy on.' Nina urged her to go ahead.

Slowly nodding, Lee turned and walked towards the conference room, but Nina could see that her senior account manager had noticed her lapses of concentration of late and Nina's propensity to lose time as her mind returned to the latest phone call, email or letter she was digesting from (a) her accountant (b) her lawyer and now (c) ASIC!

What she really wanted to do right now was crawl under the desk and hide, but that wasn't an option.

Especially not today. Sassy had become the agency's biggest earning talent, and ASIC representatives were due to speak to her at three.

Thankfully she would be supported by her lawyer, John Stacey, but the thought of meeting with officials from Australia's corporate, markets and financial services regulator made her heave with nausea. And she hadn't even done anything wrong!

Finding that she was in danger of zoning out once more, she hastily applied a bright red lipstick, finger-combed her blond curls and strode purposefully to the boardroom.

The sound of joyful laughter could be heard as she approached the doors, and in moments she was embraced in the high energy and exuberance of Sassy Swift. Yes, this woman was worth every cent, thought Nina. Look how instantly she can transform my mood!

'Nina! Hi!' Sassy engulfed her in a perfumed hug, and Nina leant into her affection. Something she didn't do with most clients, but she felt a fondness for this young woman who was beating her own drum and doing it well.

'I've ordered you a green tea,' said Lee, giving Nina a you've-got-this smile.

'Okay, so let's talk about the invitations we have for you and the five partnerships that we need to review,' said Nina, swiftly getting the meeting underway. This was when she was at her best, and for the next two hours, her worries remained far, far away.

****

The ASIC officials were every bit as intimidating as Nina had dreaded.

Calmly and methodically they explained the steps they were proceeding with in relation to her husband's business affairs. David's financial services company had been suspended from operating and would potentially be placed in receivership. One of the stern men in front of her outlined the process should it be enforced, highlighting the order of priority that would be given to her husband's vast number of creditors. Secured creditors, including the bank and Australian Taxation Office, would be first in line, as Miles had already told her, and if there was any money left over, it would then be divided among the unsecured creditors including David's clients and suppliers.

Nina's business debts wouldn't be prioritised, and their marital assets, predominantly their home, were being examined as to whether they would fall under David's financial assets and therefore needed to be sold.

It seemed that in addition to corporate receivership, David was also being pursued personally.

'We will also be potentially proceeding with criminal and civil charges against your husband in relation to corporate crime offences of falsifying information on financial statements, embezzlement and fraud,' the official stated.

'David's not a criminal,' Nina spat out, feeling a need to defend her husband.

'I'm sure this is confronting to hear, Mrs Simmons, but that is at odds with the findings of our extensive investigation. We will pursue punitive actions including financial penalties and may refer the matter to the Commonwealth Director of Public Prosecutions. These are serious charges, and if your husband is convicted on criminal charges, the penalties can range from five years to ten years' imprisonment.'

Nina sat stunned and later couldn't remember seeing the ASIC investigators out of her office, nor her solicitor, but she must have done because she found herself alone and the light fading outside her window.

CHAPTER 73: MATTHEW
Friday 15 December

At four o'clock on Friday afternoon, an email pinged from the Department of Forensic Medicine confirming what Matthew had been waiting for.

There was scientific evidence that Maddy had been in Delia Evan's SUV. A blond hair strand extracted during Reynor's thorough search of the vehicle had been analysed and was a DNA match to Maddy.

The SUV was still being held in the Cooma Police compound and would remain there following the important discovery.

As expected, Moses's DNA was also found in the vehicle, but given his mother's statement that both sons sometimes drove the vehicle, it wouldn't have been enough to go with.

The grainy image of the SUV driver lifted from the Mount Kosciusko camera had been enhanced; however, it wasn't possible to be certain of the person's identity. All that could be truthfully revealed was of a person wearing a dark-coloured baseball cap and sunglasses. It could be Moses, but it could be anyone. Male or female.

Moses's DNA wasn't found on either of the cigarette stubs found at the fire trail.

But an important part of the puzzle was now in place.

Maddy had been inside the vehicle.

'Pick him up, Davies, and take Sorenson,' announced Devens formidably. 'Crime Scene Investigation will meet you there.' A thorough examination of the flat, both vehicles and the surrounding neighbourhood would be undertaken immediately.

'Calucci? My office. Let's get this prick.'

Matthew followed Devens, and together they worked through the material they had and their line of questioning.

****

Moses's casual manner and smart-arse quips had gone, now replaced by a wariness as if he were weighing up what they knew or didn't know.

Dressed in work boots, navy cargo shorts and a black T-shirt bearing the name WeWork Plumbing, he sat stiffly at the table, accompanied by a young solicitor.

'Moses Galvin, you have been brought in for questioning in relation to the murder of Madeline Bright,' began Devens, who then proceeded to caution him.

'What? I haven't done anything!' he croaked out before Matthew explained in detail from the evidence they had collected.

A witness had confirmed that Moses's mother's SUV had been parked outside his flat on Friday 3

November, and multiple traffic cameras had spotted the vehicle driving across the Sydney Harbour Tunnel, M5 and into Mount Kosciusko National Park on that day.

Positive DNA matches for both Moses and Maddy were found inside the grey SUV.

Moses's earnest lawyer had been scribbling furiously and now requested time alone to speak with his client.

When Matthew and Devens returned a short time later, the gravity of Moses's situation had finally hit home. He was slumped forward, visibly crumbling as he shook his head left and right in vigorous denial or disbelief at being caught.

'I didn't,' he stammered, first looking at his solicitor, who offered no comment, before turning to Matthew and Devens. 'I… I… I didn't mean it!'

'What *didn't you mean*?' Matthew asked.

But Moses's response was a low groan as he held his head and began to shake uncontrollably.

'Let's start at the beginning, hey? When did you last see Madeline?' Devens asked in a calm fatherlike tone.

Moses eventually looked up, and at his solicitor's grim nod, wiped his face and began to talk. 'Ummm… yeah… in the morning at the flat.'

'That would be the morning of Friday 3 November?' Devens clarified.

'Yeah.'

'Okay. Where exactly did you see Madeline that morning?'

'She was in the shower. I didn't realise… I swear! I thought it was Jake, yeah? So I went in to take a piss.'

'Seriously?' Matthew muttered, but loud enough to be heard.

'I did!' Moses protested. 'She just freaked out.'

'What do you mean, freaked out,' Devens asked quietly.

'I, ahh, well, when I saw it was her in the shower, I sort of just joked, you know? I said I could come in, you know, join her. Wash her back.'

'Join her in the shower,' Devens continued whilst Matthew sat seething at the smarmy bastard.

'Yeah. But I was only kidding, right?' Moses now directed his responses to Devens, as if finding some understanding in the detective's non-judgemental tone.

'So, what happened?'

'Well, like I said, she sort of freaked out, yeah. Yelled and stuff. So I just left.'

'What happened next?' Devens said.

'I was in the kitchen, getting cereal and stuff, and she came in to get her keys and leave, so I went to apologise.'

'How?' Matthew asked, impatient to get the story told.

'You know.'

'No, that's why I'm asking.' Matthew swallowed his frustration.

'I tried to give her a hug, you know, and said "all good", but she pushed me away and then she yelled at me.' Moses was genuinely hurt, offended that his attempts to smooth things over with Jake's girlfriend hadn't worked.

'What did she say to you, Moses?' Devens's quiet voice probed.

'That I was always *trying it on*. That she was sick of it and was going to tell Jake. Make things up about me. I just lost it. I didn't mean to.' He swallowed, looking at them both.

'So, what happened next?' Devens's monotone questioning coaxed Moses along.

'I just wanted her to stop saying things about me. I only wanted her to stop talking.'

'How did you stop her?' Matthew held his breath as he waited for Moses to answer Devens's question and confess.

'I didn't mean to kill her!' he blurted, banging the table angrily with his fist.

His solicitor leaned over to whisper in his ear before announcing that they would require a short break.

Matthew didn't mind. They had finally got the confession.

Over four more hours the story unfolded. Moses explained that once he realised he had killed Maddy, he panicked and didn't know what to do.

'But you had the sense to call in sick at work, right?' Matthew said.

'Yeah,' he mumbled back.

Moses didn't want Jake to find out, so he had to tidy up the flat, which meant getting Maddy out of there.

He went to the garage where he found some tarpaulin and used it to wrap up Maddy's body and grabbed a shovel in case he needed to dig a hole, which then got him thinking of where, eventually settling on Mount Kosciusko.

'I had Mum's car and knew she had the annual pass,' he said, referring to her Kosciusko permit.

He then drove the five-hundred-kilometre trip to Thredbo in less than six hours. He recalled the various fire trails on the mountain from his previous visits and picked one that he thought would be passable, given there was still some snow around. He then carried Maddy, still wrapped in the tarp on his shoulder, like a sack, to an area remote enough to bury her. A place where she wouldn't be discovered for some time. Or so he thought.

He unwrapped her from the tarp and buried her in a shallow grave, careful to take back the shovel and tarp, which he burnt at a secluded picnic spot about one hundred kilometres from Cooma.

When he got back to the flat at around ten, Jake was watching basketball, and he joined him on the sofa. Like nothing had happened. Nothing at all.

CHAPTER 74: LOUISE
Sunday 17 December

The town of Bundanoon was more a village really, and as Theodore steered the car slowly around the bend in the main street, Louise watched the small parade of people moving along the pavement.

'Oh, there's a market on!' exclaimed Louise, before remembering that they weren't there for a weekend drive, but rather they were about to drop Chloe for two weeks of rehab.

Neither Theodore nor a stony-faced Chloe in the back seat commented, and Louise focused her attention on the GPS, trying to offer something more constructive to their solemn drive to the retreat.

About five minutes on, they turned off and headed away from the bustling village through quiet suburban streets that then transformed into open countryside with larger sprawling properties. And there she was.

Huntington Retreat.

The name on the austere gates announced they had arrived, and the long drive up to the main entrance only served to increase the tension that was now palpable inside the car.

Louise thought she might be sick, but she needed to remain upbeat and strong for Chloe. She fumbled for her lipstick and applied a thick coat to add much-needed colour to her now pale features before alighting from the car.

'This looks pretty nice, hey Chloe,' Theodore said, pulling his daughter in under his arm.

'Yeah, I guess,' Chloe mumbled, her eyes slowly scanning their surrounds.

'Welcome. Welcome!' A cheery middle-aged woman strode towards them from the side of the building.

Introducing herself as Nancy Shepherd, the Duty Manager, she offered them a warm, encouraging smile.

'I've set up coffee and tea just over on the side patio if you'd like to join me?'

'Sure,' said Louise in an upbeat voice, relieved to have someone to ease them into this.

They followed Nancy around the building into a small courtyard where several wicker chairs and a table were set up with small sandwiches and what looked like a home-made slice.

After pouring teas and coffees, Nancy began to explain the history of Huntington Retreat.

Her calming voice and her endeavours to engage with each of them were reassuring. She had no doubt had much practice in greeting overwhelmed parents and frightened teenagers.

Nancy made no reference to Chloe's purpose for staying, only to assure her that she would find the property both restorative and calming.

Louise pondered asking for a second room, because right now that combination sounded like heaven.

CHAPTER 75: MATTHEW

The paperwork was never ending, and Matthew stood up to stretch his tired shoulders.

Moses had been charged with murder, and Matthew suspected the Director of Public Prosecutions would reduce the charge to manslaughter. There wasn't significant evidence to prove an obvious intent to kill Maddy that morning, instead a reckless indifference that when Moses grabbed her throat to ostensibly shut her up, he had cruelly suffocated her.

It had been a huge relief for Matthew and the team when Moses was led away to the police van, knowing that he would pay for taking her young life. Matthew had appreciated the praise Devens fielded his way in being the first in the small detective team to catch on to Moses as the key person of interest.

'I like your instinct, Matthew. Serves you well. If you're interested in staying on after filing the brief, of course, I'd like to keep you,' Devens had said, cornering Matthew in the dark pub the night before. Something he definitely intended to think about.

For the past twenty-four hours, Matthew had immersed himself in preparing the brief of evidence for the Director of Public Prosecutions. On Monday he would meet with the DPP's senior Crown prosecutor and assisting solicitors to provide an initial overview, and he didn't want the case to fall over at the outset because he hadn't documented something correctly.

Moses was refused bail on the strength of the Crown case, which included the scientific evidence and now confession, and he would be back in front of the Courts in three months time. His trial would be at least twelve months away.

Matthew decided to wander down and get a coffee and was just exiting the lift when his mobile phone pinged.

Looking down at his screen, he saw a new email from Mountain Ski Resort.

After placing his coffee order, he opened the message, but the font was too small to read clearly, so he impatiently waited to collect his coffee so he could return upstairs to read it properly.

Hurrying back to his desk, Matthew opened the email and saw an attachment, the report he had requested of Moses's snowboarding students from three years back. When he opened the document, his eyes quickly scanned the two hundred names, some of whom were repeated, and there she was. Ella Williams.

His heart stopped.

A link.

Could the same scumbag be responsible for the young woman's disappearance and possible murder?

CHAPTER 76: ANNE-MARIE
Monday 18 December

Anne-Marie stood back on the pavement to admire the two shops, New Age Jewels and her baby sister, Bespoke Bling. Louise had chosen the cute name to christen the new workshop space.

'I'm so impressed!' She gave Louise a tight squeeze.

'Well, just wait until you see inside. I just love the space, and I'm sure you will too,' Louise gushed.

It was heart-warming to see Louise's smiling dimples reappear and hear the happiness return to her voice. Anne-Marie had been worried about Lou after learning about her daughter's close call with drugs. Since Chloe had been admitted to the Southern Highlands retreat, Louise was much more like her old, chilled self again.

'I just feel relieved that she's got a team of people around her who know what to say, how to help. And she has other people with her who are going through something similar, so hopefully she can talk to them too.'

Opening up the double doors to the studio, Louise showed her through, and Anne-Marie admired the whitewashed and divine airy spaciousness. It was a room you wanted to spend time in, and she said as much to Lou.

Colourful red and silver tinsel had been hung from each of the long white benches, and a real Christmas tree stood in the corner, delivering a woody pine scent to the room, which had been sealed up overnight. The fragrance was soothing and intoxicating.

'I love it!' Anne-Marie said. 'I want to sign up to a workshop please!'

'Well, maybe if we manage the Christmas frenzy next door,' Lou said, smiling back at her.

'Ahhh yes, you better show me the ropes so I'm not completely useless this week.' Anne-Marie had worked in her fair share of retail shops in her youth, and with a few clear instructions from Lou, she would be up and running in no time.

Closing up the studio and entering the shop, Louise dumped her bags in the back office whilst Anne-Marie roamed the floor to peruse the cabinets.

The jewellery displays were magical, each cabinet drawing her to a different theme. Retro, antique and vintage pieces were housed along one side of the floor, and contemporary costume pieces along another. In the centre of the room were the more expensive items, which Louise was now setting up. Stunning pearl necklaces and drop earrings were being placed into their designated spots, and an array of exquisite diamond and coloured stones continued to flow out of the safe and be assembled in velvet cases.

'These are the real gems,' Louise said, laying out a matching set of sapphire and crystal earrings and a long intricate necklace.

'We now have around thirty designers sending in their pieces, and they are unbelievably beautiful. Imagine wearing this to a Christmas party or on New

Year's Eve,' Lou said, still fingering the sparkling blue creation.

It was soon time to flick over the OPEN sign, and within ten minutes the first customer had arrived, a middle-aged man in a business suit who looked overwhelmed when the front door closed behind him and he found both Anne-Marie and Louise watching him.

'Can I help you?' Louise gave him one of her awesome full dimple smiles.

'I'm just looking for something for my wife,' the man mumbled, gazing around anxiously.

'Perhaps if you tell me what sort of jewellery your wife likes to wear, we can find the perfect piece together.' Louise's voice was nurturing and kind, and she led the man around the shop, pointing out various pieces until he settled on an antique broach.

Ringing up the sale and farewelling the customer, Louise went back to tweak her displays whilst Anne-Marie felt a surge of pride in her friend's ability to be so gentle and caring when she was grappling with her own problems.

Half an hour later, two women in Lycra arrived, clutching coffees and browsing, and minutes later another woman arrived, pushing a stroller.

The traffic continued at a steady pace all day, and despite a few coffees and sandwich runs, Louise and Anne-Marie were busy on their feet for the whole day.

'At least Jules will be in tomorrow,' Louise said, giving her a reassuring smile. 'Her kids are on school holidays so she can only manage a few hours each day, but that will be something.'

'Too right!' Anne-Marie agreed, letting out an exaggerated sigh.

When the store was closed and the precious jewels stored away, Anne-Marie gratefully sat down with Louise in the back office and watched as she processed the day's takings.

Slipping her heels out of her wedge slingbacks, Anne-Marie massaged her aching feet and leant back in the worn but comfortable recliner.

'Hey, don't get too comfy over there, love. I'm taking you for aperols to celebrate. We just sold $15,000—a record for a Monday!'

'Woo hoo!' Anne-Marie cheered, beaming with pleasure at having played a part in the day's success.

'Come on, get those shoes back on. Drinks are on me!'

CHAPTER 77: MATTHEW
Wednesday 20 December

Within two days, a search team had been mobilised at Mount Kosciusko.

Matthew had been gratified that Devens had immediately agreed to get the crew up there.

Standing now at the familiar fire trail, which had netted them results in the Madeline Bright case, Matthew looked at the faces of the five police officers who had been recruited from the Jindabyne and Cooma stations and the six members of the National Parks and Wildlife Service.

Matthew explained the background on the eighteen-month-old case, although most of the officers and rangers knew the details of Ella Williams's disappearance all too well. Some of the men looking back at him had been involved in the initial search and looked as desperate as he was to find out what happened.

Regardless, he recapped the snowboarder's last known movements on the final day of her family's week-long stay at Thredbo.

'Ella was a strong snowboarder, and her father said that she especially liked two ski runs,' Matthew explained, highlighting them on the large map laid out on a table before them all.

'We'll divide into three crews—so mix up with each other. I want police and National Parks working together on this. The first two groups will tackle the ski runs, and the third will focus around here and the site of Maddy Bright's grave.'

'I want the dog unit to start here first,' he said, looking at the police officer and his four-legged companion.

Matthew distributed colour print-outs of the clothing items that Ella was wearing prior to her last sighting—the vivid pink ski jacket and ski goggles and black ski pants and helmet.

'Any sign of these items, call it in,' he insisted. 'Any trace of her, I want to know.'

Matthew would stay in the makeshift HQ with the head ranger, Guy Swan, who knew every inch of Kosciusko and would be a huge asset when strategising other potential search areas.

Detective Sorenson was en route from Sydney and would assist Matthew in the coordination efforts when she arrived.

Hours later, the crews had returned in dribs and drabs without anything to show for the time they had spent combing the mountain.

Was Matthew's instinct off?

'Okay, we'll get going again in the morning when the light is better,' Matthew announced to the weary crews, injecting more hope than he felt.

After farewelling Guy and the dispirited NP&WS crew, Matthew, Sorenson and the officers drove their assorted vehicles into Thredbo for the night.

CHAPTER 78: NINA

The invitation to drinks couldn't have been timed better. Not long after parting ways with her staff at their lavish Christmas lunch at the swanky Café CBD, Nina was strolling back to the office.

She had some final emails she wanted to send before switching on her computer's auto reply message and officially logging off for two weeks.

After Christmas she was contemplating visiting the renowned health retreat in Queensland's Tallebudgera Valley that her old family friends owned. They had been inviting her to visit for ages, and right now she was in dire need of a quiet place to take stock. Nina needed a sure-fire way to unwind, recalibrate and restore her equilibrium for the challenges awaiting her in the year ahead.

Her smartwatch vibrated alerting her to an incoming call, and glancing down, she saw Dermott's name on the small screen. She retrieved her phone from her handbag.

'Nina, I wanted to see if you were still in the city and fancied a Christmas drink?'

Nina's heart flipped at the timely invitation, because right now a festive drink was exactly what she wanted.

Arranging to meet at the lobby bar at Dermott's hotel in half an hour, Nina continued on to her office where she hastily refreshed her face with concealer and mascara before attending to the emails.

Activating the Out of Office function on her inbox, she switched on the answering machine and locked the front door. She was now officially on holidays, and it felt liberating.

Dermott was sitting at a low table in the centre of the buzzing lobby bar when Nina arrived, and he rose to greet her with a light kiss to each cheek.

'You look lovely as always,' he said, waiting for her to sit down first.

'Thanks, Dermott, but I doubt that's true,' she said, all too aware of the toll the past month had taken on her appearance. Those easy breezy days in Tahiti seemed like a lifetime ago. She was way too skinny, and if not for the make-up now plastered all over her gaunt face, she would look frightfully pale and pinched as well.

Ordering drinks, the conversation flowed, initially covering their mutual campaign with Sassy Swift and Craylee before turning to the purpose of Dermott's Sydney visit.

'Clients!' He gave her lopsided grin. 'This is the busiest time of the year for the wine industry, which is why I'm drinking a beer tonight! But don't tell my bosses that.' He laughed.

'When do you head back to Adelaide?' She took a sip of her rosé and savoured its sweetness.

'In the morning, and then I'll take a decent break after the Christmas-New Year frenzy is done. We've got some major scale promotions around New Year's

Eve, client hospitality events and international VIPs to host first.'

Nina didn't envy what sounded like a hectic schedule, her tense shoulders relaxed slightly, knowing she was now on leave. She didn't have anything to do except rest and recharge.

'I'm pondering a wellness retreat in early January. A friend owns a gorgeous property in Queensland and has been inviting me to stay forever,' she said.

'I thought you were skiing in Aspen?'

Her dreamy smile had evaporated instantly.

'Shit! Sorry!' Dermott hastily backpedalled. 'I didn't mean to upset you.'

Before she knew it, Nina was biting back a tsunami of tears. Dermott quickly handed over a crisp handkerchief, which she gratefully clutched.

'Why don't I get a table for dinner,' he murmured, moving away to speak to the maître d'. Nina used the time to compose herself, dabbing at her shiny cheeks and smudged eyes, before checking herself in her compact.

'I've got a nice quiet table for us,' he said, reappearing to escort her into the calm ambience of the restaurant.

Two hours later over several bottles of fine wine and a small salad for her and a large steak for Dermott, Nina revealed her woes.

It was a relief to offload her worrying thoughts, and Dermott proved to be a good listener. Sympathy and compassion oozed out of him. Reaching for her hand, he squeezed it gently. 'You will get through this, Nina.'

It was much-needed reassurance, Dermott's confidence seeping into her tired, fragile state of mind.

She shared her idea of retreating to the luxury resort for a week and discovered that Dermott had been to the property, several times in fact. He encouraged her to go.

'Just give up coffee beforehand,' he warned. 'Believe me, you'll be glad of it when you realise there's no caffeine on a detox retreat.'

'Noted,' she said, smiling her thanks. He had lifted her spirits in more ways than he knew.

CHAPTER 79: MATTHEW

Matthew had showered and was relishing the first mouthful of beer from the minibar when his mobile rang.

It was Guy Swan. 'Matthew, I've got a thought on another location we could look at tomorrow.'

Matthew turned the television down so he could listen as the head ranger explained a whole new theory about where Ella Williams could be.

A short time later Matthew strode into the hotel bar to meet Sorenson, finding her at the counter, chatting with a bug-eyed bartender. Breaking up their conversation, he ordered beers and indicated they should grab a secluded table at the rear. The young man's face dropped a little as Sorenson was wrenched away from their cosy tête-à-tête.

'So, an interesting development from Guy Swan just now,' Matthew began after they had settled into the booth. 'There's an area on the western side of the mountain that he said we should look at.'

'Accessible by road?' she asked, taking a sip of the beer.

'Yes and no. We can drive in, but then it's a good twenty-minute walk across to the site, maybe longer.'

'Why there?'

'Apparently the area has been relatively inaccessible for two to three years now. Huge dumps of snow, followed by rock falls in the summer, and the cycle continues. Guy said the mountain face has changed because of the force of it all, and it would be the perfect hidey hole.' Matthew grimaced at his flippant expression, but Sorenson would know he wasn't being deliberately callous.

They stayed on to split a pizza, and Matthew ordered another round of drinks. He enjoyed Sorenson's company and could understand why the man pouring their drinks had looked bereft at her earlier departure.

For someone so young—just twenty six years old—Sorenson had a maturity beyond her years, and that included her approach to values, ethics and her personal affairs. Her partner, Tyler, was a physiotherapist, and Matthew envied the tight bond and deep love they obviously shared. Sorenson's face radiated pure happiness when she talked about Tyler and their plans to get married and raise a family.

If only he had taken the time to discuss shared values and life goals when he had married Monica so long ago. If they had, perhaps they wouldn't have ended up as another couple in Australia's spiralling divorce rates.

Matthew had felt like a failure when his marriage had soured, Monica resenting the time he gave his police work and the reduced wage he was now bringing home. She had signed up to marry a lawyer, something she had repeated more times than he cared to remember, as if she had been unfairly duped when he had decided he had had enough of law and wanted to work on the other side of law enforcement.

Monica married his colleague within twelve months of their divorce, and Matthew hoped she was enjoying the comforts he had so abruptly denied her.

CHAPTER 80: ANNE-MARIE
Thursday 21 December

'Hello?' Anne-Marie answered her phone tentatively. She was suspicious of unknown numbers, which more often than not ended up being enthusiastic telemarketers trying to convince her to switch energy suppliers or compare mobile phone plans.

'Hello, is that Ms Christenson?' a crisp female voice asked before proceeding to introduce herself as Naomi Cruickshank, phoning from Ziggy Annear's office.

That caught Anne-Marie's instant attention. Ziggy Annear was one of the country's most successful businessmen with a wealth exceeding billions of dollars. Not only was he a mining magnate, but he was also the nation's most generous philanthropist together with his wife Helen and adult family.

The caller was oblivious to the awe Anne-Marie was experiencing at the other end of the line and continued on briskly. 'I am telephoning to schedule a Zoom meeting with Mr Annear, if possible, tomorrow?'

'Ummm. Sorry, I'm not sure if you have the right person?' Anne-Marie said, bamboozled by the call. *What meeting?* Why would she have a meeting with a man like Ziggy Annear? Surely there was some mistake.

'Oh, I'm so sorry!' Naomi sounded mortified, and Anne-Marie was anticipating that this was when the woman would admit her error. She would confess that she had meant to phone Jane Christenson, or Emily Christenson or any other Christenson than Anne-Marie.

'I should have explained at the outset. The meeting is in relation to the position you applied for to be Mr Annear's private travel and lifestyle manager.'

Anne-Marie had applied for seven or eight jobs in the past two weeks, and her mind whirred quickly across each of them. She would have definitely remembered applying for a job with Ziggy Annear.

And then the penny dropped. Her mind zeroed in on the mysterious role that had looked too good to be true.

PRIVATE TRAVEL AND LIFESTYLE MANAGER

"An experienced professional specialising in the fields of travel and executive assistance is sought by a private business to commence immediately. Your role would be to coordinate all travel requirements for an executive client and manage a highly complex diary and schedule. Must be highly organised, efficient and discreet."

'Oh, of course!' Anne-Marie cried with relief, as if she had just figured out the riddle. 'I applied via a recruitment company, so I wasn't expecting a direct call.'

'No problem,' Naomi chirped. 'Mr Annear was impressed with your application and has requested an interview tomorrow morning at eleven if that is possible? Sorry it's late notice, but he would be most grateful if you were available.'

Anne-Marie almost shouted YES in her haste to secure the meeting.

If only to meet such an impressive individual.

CHAPTER 81: MATTHEW

The following morning Matthew arrived at the hotel dining room to find Sorenson and Guy settled at a large table with coffees. Pouring himself one and grabbing a croissant from the basket of pastries, he joined them.

As they chatted and checked their emails, the room quickly filled with local police officers and park rangers for the early briefing.

Once everyone was seated with coffee, Matthew and Guy walked to the front of the room.

'Good morning and thank you for your efforts yesterday,' Matthew began. 'Today we will be searching the back country on the western side, known as "The Ledge". It's infamous among avid snowboarders and skiers.'

Matthew pointed to the area on the large map fixed on the wall behind him.

'We are pursuing two lines of investigation. The first, that Ella struck difficulty, potentially resulting in a fatal fall. And the second, that someone knew about this area and had a reason to use the torrid geography to their advantage. To conceal a body.'

He handed over to Guy to expand on the region.

'The Ledge is a notorious jumping-off spot for adventure skiers and boarders each winter. Some of you will recall the blizzard of 2017. Since then, this area'—Guy circled a small section of the map—'has become increasingly unstable with follow-up snow dumps annually and rock falls in summer. Crevasses have emerged. It's a definite no-go site for the public, which unfortunately makes it highly appealing to backcountry skiers.'

Guy highlighted on the map where the closest road was, another fire trail, and the best route to walk across to the notorious ledge, before Matthew issued a stern warning.

'It's extremely tricky and dangerous terrain, and we could be out there all day, so take jackets, satellite phones, GPS, torches, first aid… all the mandatory equipment. It might be getting to twenty-two degrees today, but it won't feel like it up there, so warm gear and jackets are essential. Lunch bags and water are on the table, so grab yours on the way out. Let's go!'

Within an hour, the group was eagerly assembled at the western fire trail, and the head ranger began leading the way.

On the western side, the landscape was much harsher than Matthew had anticipated. The backcountry terrain was treacherous, and one slip could prove fatal with the gleaming rock faces beckoning far below. Exposed ridges and patches of snow clung resolutely.

If Ella had been snowboarding here, Matthew could see how unforgiving the ground would be to any misstep. Steep boulders and stomach-curdling cliffs were laid out before him. The sound was eery, as the wind reverberated up the cliffs, mimicking strangled cries and moaning.

'This area is the last to thaw out on the mountain, due in part to the shadow that falls across here from above and the wind tunnel that cuts through here,' explained Guy.

Matthew could feel the chill creeping through his sweater as the sun failed to win the battle to shine over the landscape.

'The ground cover never clears of snow completely. This year is warmer than the past few, so it gives us a good opportunity to have a look around,' Guy explained.

The blanket cover had diminished substantially but there was still a lot of snow about.

'The thick snow is the appeal. Powder plus being off piste equals bragging rights.' Guy shook his head sadly, as if to say, *What can you do?'*

The walking became slow and tricky. There was no path, and the terrain was uneven and awkward to navigate, forcing them to crouch down to jump from surface to surface whilst avoiding ankle-twisting holes and knee-breaking gaps in the rocks. As Matthew turned a bend in the mountain, the Ledge came into view, rising above them in all its danger and majesty.

Like its name sounded, the Ledge jutted out off the mountain and provided an ideal launch pad if you were confident on the landing zone below. But the soft snow that had once cushioned a snowboard or set of skis was gone now, and rocks, boulders and rugged earth revealed the force of mother nature.

Guy had recommended they approach from below. 'If Ella skied over the cliff, we'll invariably find evidence as we begin our ascent.'

Police and rangers broke into pairs to cautiously comb the rock faces and look for anything that would signify a human's presence. The only sound Matthew could hear as he and Guy walked slowly upward was the eerie call of the wind as it flung around the ragged cliffs.

'Some backcountry skiers have sworn they've heard voices out this way,' Guy said after Matthew commented on the strangled sound.

Matthew could understand why. The wind wasn't overly fierce, but it was strong enough to reduce the temperature considerably and create a haunting cry and disturbing groan from time to time.

For the next few hours, they silently worked their way up, inching across the rugged environment, and Matthew was about to call time for everyone to take a break and recharge, when a yell was heard.

The panicked voice of one of the young officers got the rest of them scrambling with renewed energy upward to reach him.

Matthew was among the first to get there. He had sprinted to reach the site and was now buckled over catching his breath trying to take in the view.

He narrowed his gaze, and there, suspended between two boulders, was what looked like a pile of discarded ski gear, but if you looked more closely, the reality of the scene became distressingly apparent. The pink was unmistakeable.

CHAPTER 82: ANNE-MARIE
Friday 22 December

'Good morning,' Anne-Marie said nervously, her eyes darting across her laptop screen, trying to work out who to look at as three serious strangers stared back at her expectantly. Suddenly realising they couldn't hear her, she fumbled with the Zoom microphone switch and silently cursed her ineptness.

'Sorry. Hi!' Her heartbeat was up in her throat, but she was determined not to betray how flustered she felt.

'Anne-Marie. Thank you for joining us,' boomed a deep voice from the man in the middle, who then gave her an enormous smile. She recognised him instantly as the high-profile mining magnate Ziggy Annear.

'I've got my head of personnel here, Terry Blake, and my executive assistant, Naomi Cruickshank, who I believe you have spoken with.'

'Yes, hi. Hello.' She nodded at each of them and earned a weak smile from Naomi and an eye blink from Terry.

Anne-Marie refused to be put off by the blank stares from the other two, and after some awkward small talk, Ziggy steered the focus to her professional background. Anne-Marie's answers to the first few questions were stilted before she eventually found her rhythm and began expanding on her experience in corporate travel, the software systems she had mastered and her proficiency in managing her past client's travel schedules. She even managed to elicit a few smiles.

'So, what happened with your previous role at Executive Traveller?' asked Tony, intensely scrutinising her.

Anne-Marie was about to brush away the question with something like '*Oh, I just felt the time was right for a new opportunity blah blah blah*', but hesitated. If Ziggy Annear's team hadn't done their due diligence on her, she doubted they would be on staff.

'I had been working there for seven years and wanted more autonomy and responsibility,' she said simply.

'Well, that's just what I'm looking for!' boomed Ziggy, giving her an appraising nod and essentially closing down that line of questioning, much to Anne-Marie's relief.

****

That evening over dinner, Anne-Marie recounted the interview to Louise and Theodore. She needed to debrief and hear their reassurance, because she had been doubting herself all day, wishing she could redo the whole thing.

'The salary and bonus package is phenomenal. The role is just what I want—in-house, only executive and luxury personal travel arrangements for the Annear family business, six weeks annual leave, flexible work arrangements. Did I mention the salary package? I really want it,' she moaned dramatically, as Louise patted her hand.

'It sounds like you did really well. Stop beating yourself up about it. You would be just perfect!'

'Well, hopefully I'll hear either way before Christmas or at least by New Year's,' Anne-Marie said, although she wouldn't hold her breath knowing that most businesses were winding down for a two- or three-week holiday. But how long could she hold out without an income? Would she have to take one of those crummy travel agency roles she saw advertised? Please no!

CHAPTER 83: MATTHEW

A pair of forensically trained crime scene investigators arrived at eight o'clock the next morning. It had been too late for them to land the helicopter the day before, and one more day wasn't going to make a huge difference at this stage.

Matthew was convinced it was Ella.

Two police officers in the group had volunteered to do the overnight shift on the mountain to preserve the scene, and Guy organised protective equipment and food for them whilst Matthew and Sorenson travelled with the rest of the crew back into the village for the night.

Matthew instantly grinned seeing Reynor alight from the chopper.

'You said this was out of your league,' Matthew said on shaking Reynor's hand.

'Yes, but I'm in good company.' He indicated the two CSIs powering ahead of them. 'Plus I didn't want to miss any possible connection—you mentioned a potential link between the two cases?'

Matthew had explained his theory to Reynor when he had called in the discovery, but after spending the best part of two hours talking with the rangers, he now wasn't so sure.

'It's notorious backcountry here. More than a few experienced skiers strike difficulty,' one of the seasoned volunteers told Matthew during their long wait. 'If you end up with a broken leg, you've done well.'

Could Ella have struck difficulty and injured herself? Or worse, fallen off the cliff to her death?

'Another theory is that she struck trouble, the weather was coming in and she huddled down into the snow?' suggested Guy Swan. 'But she would need a lot of experience to know how to build a snow cave, and for a sixteen-year-old, I just don't buy it.'

Matthew had read about the case of four American snowboarders who had disappeared on the mountain back in 1999. They weren't found until the arrival of spring, months later, their bodies revealed in the last vestiges of a snow cave. The theory at the time was that the men had suffocated because their ventilation hole had frozen over and the sheer amount of snowfall had tragically buried them alive.

Or could the explanation be found on the northern beaches of Sydney in the name of Moses Galvin?

CHAPTER 84: LOUISE
Saturday 23 December

Louise had just wrapped up her final Christmas baubles workshop two days before Christmas, and the series had been a whopping success. It had sparked wonderful creativity, a lot of laughter and generated some of her heftiest sales that month. It had also proven to be a good distraction from thinking about Chloe.

Louise had needed the change of pace and a way for her to channel her energy, and she felt reassured knowing that Anne-Marie, and Jules too, were next door attending to her customers.

Anne-Marie had been a godsend. It had been Louise's busiest Christmas ever, and without her dear friend's support—both in the shop and emotionally at home—she wouldn't have got through it.

The workshops had gone extremely well. Fifteen budding designers in attendance at each session, hanging on to her every instruction and creating the most fabulous jewellery pieces from Christmas-inspired red, green and silver earrings to leather and wire necklaces and beaded bracelets, and dangly baubles for the Christmas tree.

Louise had enjoyed connecting with her regulars as well as meeting new faces, who she hoped she would see a lot more of in the New Year. But for now, she was taking a well-earned break over the Christmas and New Year's period.

'Hey, are you ready to go?' Anne-Marie asked, popping her head into the studio.

'Sure am.' Lou smiled, turning off the lights for the last time for two weeks.

After locking up both doors, Anne-Marie put her arm through Louise's and steered her down the street to the wine bar they had been frequenting most nights for a festive tipple before heading home.

In minutes, they were seated at their regular high table, and just as Louise was about to grab her purse, she gave a shriek.

'Surprise!' Nina cried, swiftly enveloping Louise in a hug before doing the same to Anne-Marie.

'My goodness, Nina! I can't believe you're here!'

The last Louise knew was that Nina was going to be away skiing over Christmas.

'But what happened?' she blustered, looking at Nina for an explanation.

'Did you know?' Louise quickly eyeballed Anne-Marie, who grinned before heading to the bar.

'I wanted to be here with you.' Nina gave her a bright smile. 'How's Chloe?'

'She seems to be doing okay. We can't see her of course, but we get regular updates and she's settled in really well and making progress.' Louise gave a sad sigh.

'I'm really glad, and just think she will be back with you in no time.' Nina hugged her again.

'All right, girls, look what we have here,' said Anne-Marie, returning with an ice bucket containing a bottle of Veuve Cliquot and three chilled flutes balanced around the bottle.

'We are celebrating tonight. It's Christmas and the girls are back together again!' Anne-Marie poured them each a generous glass and then raised hers to them both.

'Here's to a much-needed holiday,' Anne-Marie said, looking at each of them.

'And a happier year than the one we've just had,' Nina jumped in.

'One with no more dramas!' Louise chorused.

'Cheers!' They clinked their glasses and drank.

CHAPTER 85: NINA
Sunday 24 December

Waking up at Louise's home was peaceful, and Nina surrendered into the quiet before eventually throwing off the silky sheets and walking to the shower.

She was staying in Chloe's old childhood room, and although the teenage posters and paraphernalia had been stored away when Chloe moved out at the start of the year, traces remained. A wardrobe of funky clothes and a dresser brimming with cosmetics, colourful jewellery and an assortment of photos. Evidence of her return to home after a year of independence.

Nina felt a pang of sadness as she looked at Chloe's fresh face, so full of happiness and laughter as she pouted for the camera with her girlfriends, the four women looking much older and more sophisticated than their teenage years. Beside it sat a large image of Chloe grinning at her high school graduation, framed by the protective arms of her proud parents.

Nina felt a deep sorrow for Chloe, Louise and Theodore and this trial they were enduring. Lou and Chloe had always had such a close mother and daughter relationship, and at times it seemed like they were more like sisters. Swapping make-up and clothes, going away for indulgent weekends together at glamourous Sydney hotels, and sharing intimacies. It would have been awful for Lou to have seen Chloe so near death and to realise that she didn't know what was going on in her own daughter's life.

Sometimes it was the person who was closest to you who had the biggest secrets to keep. She knew that only too well.

Shrugging off the unpleasant thoughts of her deceitful husband, she ran a brush through her hair and went downstairs for breakfast, finding Louise and Anne-Marie chatting on the kitchen bench.

'Morning sleepyhead,' said Anne-Marie, giving her a cheeky smile.

Nina sat down on the empty stool beside her, and Louise made her a pot of green tea.

'Our Christmas Eve tradition is usually having the neighbours and a few friends over for cocktails, but with everything that's been happening, I haven't organised it this year,' Louise said.

'Well, we're friends and we're here!' Anne-Marie said, full of good spirits this morning.

'Unless you don't feel up to it?' Nina added cautiously.

'No, I'd actually love to inject more cheer back into the house,' Louise admitted. 'Let's do it!' She went to find her phone to spread the word.

An hour later, the three women arrived at Canberra Central to embark on some last-minute Christmas shopping as well as source the supplies for this evening's impromptu soirée. The crowded car park was the first clue that they weren't the only ones doing some late gift buying, but Nina relished the buzz.

The manic energy of frantic shoppers was intoxicating. The reality that it was Christmas Eve brought a joyful smile to her face. And best of all, she had these two wonderful friends to hang out with.

****

'I think that's the last one!' Louise sounded triumphant at wrapping the final spinach-and-ricotta triangle, placing it on the large tray on the kitchen table.

'And the mini quiches are ready too,' Nina announced, sitting back to admire the three dozen tartelettes monopolising the other half of their workspace.

Anne-Marie was in the lounge room, hanging the extra Christmas decorations and moving furniture with Theodore to accommodate this evening's small crowd. An assortment of glassware had been set up on a table just outside the back door, with large tubs ready to be filled with ice, wine and beer.

Louise and Theodore were clearly popular; they had eighteen people confirmed for tonight.

With the preparation now complete, Nina and the others went upstairs to shower and change and were all assembled again downstairs when the first guest arrived.

Anne-Marie found a Christmas carols playlist on Spotify to gently waft through the speakers while Nina busied herself in the kitchen, trading baking trays in the oven. Theodore and Louise were playing gracious hosts, welcoming in a steady stream of neighbours and friends.

Leaving the kitchen, Nina paused to see her dear friend laughing with a couple by the door, and Nina felt a warm glow. She was glad she wasn't at a posh ski slope with David right now; this was exactly where she needed, and wanted, to be.

CHAPTER 86: MATTHEW

Matthew was at the Queanbeyan police headquarters, having returned from Thredbo that morning.

Ella Williams's distraught parents had positively identified her body in the Sydney morgue, and the post-mortem results had just come in. It confirmed that Ella had a fractured skull consistent with a high-impact fall, but it wasn't believed to be the cause of death.

The pathologist said she most likely died of suffocation due to being unconscious and buried in heavy snow. There was no evidence of strangulation nor of foul play.

Moses Galvin was unlikely to blame.

And that disappointed Matthew. He had wanted someone to blame for Ella's senseless death. Not for it to be because she had been young and fearless, believing herself to be invincible, as most teenagers did.

'Not much of a Christmas gift for the family, is it?' Reynor remarked to Matthew as they washed their coffee mugs in the small kitchenette.

'Nope,' Matthew agreed. 'Such a tragic waste of a young life.'

'What are your plans now?' his colleague asked.

'I'll stick around Canberra for a week or two, finalise the report on Ella Williams and then head back to Sydney for a while.'

Wishing each other a good break, Reynor left the office and Matthew returned to his desk. It was nearing seven o'clock, and he contemplated settling in for another hour or two.

The Madeline Bright brief had been drafted, and Matthew would review it one final time before it was submitted to the DPP. That wouldn't be until at least mid-January, now that the legal system—along with almost every other business and industry in the country—was on a lengthy Christmas break.

He hadn't made any plans for Christmas because he hadn't known where he would be or the stage of both investigations. But now the cases were largely wrapped up, and he would spend the holidays at his own home in Canberra.

It would be good to have time off to get the place back in order, mow the lawn, paint the deck, and maybe chill out with a good book or two.

Maybe even reach out to a few friends. Suddenly he remembered Louise's call and went to play his voicemail.

CHAPTER 87: ANNE-MARIE

The party was in full swing, and there were at least twenty-five people spread across Louise and Theodore's lounge room and back garden. The doorbell went again, and Anne-Marie was nearest, so she went to let in the final guests. Well, she assumed they would be the last, as the numbers were growing considerably by the minute!

When she opened the door, she started at seeing Matthew.

'Hi,' he emitted with surprise, giving her a quizzical look.

'Hi,' she stuttered, feeling a warm blush creep up her neck and face.

Matthew leaned in to peck her flushed cheek, politely refraining from commenting. Anne-Marie never blushed, well, not since she was about fourteen and had a mad crush on a sixteen-year-old neighbour.

'Happy Christmas. I wasn't expecting to see you here. In Canberra.'

'I'm staying with Lou and Theo for Christmas. Sorry, come on in,' she said, moving to let him pass through into the house and successfully putting some distance between them.

'I thought you were in Sydney,' she said, leading him towards the kitchen to find Louise.

'Yeah, I was, but I'm back here for Christmas. Just for a while. Hey, Louise!'

Louise looked up from the benchtop and put her oven mitts down to give Matthew a warm hug.

'Thanks for the invite,' he said and handed over a bottle of champagne he had been holding.

Anne-Marie knew she should leave the old friends to catch up, but her feet remained rooted to the kitchen floor, and she couldn't tear her eyes away from his handsome face. He had acquired a light tan since she had last seen him, and his deep brown eyes crinkled as he laughed easily with Louise.

After listening to the pair chatter for a few minutes, Anne-Marie finally felt able to move and turned to leave the kitchen.

'Hey, Anne-Marie, would you take Matthew and introduce him around?' Louise asked.

She stiffened. 'Why don't I take over in the kitchen, Lou, and you can introduce him to your friends?'

Louise's eyes lit up. 'Thanks, love!' Lou explained what needed longer in the oven and where the serving trays and napkins were, before putting her arm through Matthew's and skipping out of the room.

The kitchen seemed lonely without them, but suddenly the night had a whole lot of possibilities.

For the next ten minutes, Anne-Marie busied herself in the kitchen, taking the heated quiches, sausage rolls and triangles out of the oven when the buzzer went, and she placed them onto Louise's large serving platters. She put a new batch of each into the oven and then went out to hand around the food.

Nina offered to take one of the platters, so Anne-Marie took her time mingling and chatting with guests as they gushed over the warm treats.

'Louise has got you working,' teased Matthew when Anne-Marie came outside to the garden where he had been standing. He introduced her to the couple he had been talking to, who were mutual university friends of Louise and Matthew's, and she enjoyed hearing more about them both in their college days.

The platter was eventually discarded as Anne-Marie became engrossed in the entertaining conversation. Eventually the couple bid their farewells, and Anne-Marie and Matthew were alone.

Topping up her champagne flute and grabbing a beer from the ice bath beside them, they wandered over to sit on the deck chairs spread around the garden where dainty fairy lights lit up the trees.

'Sorry I haven't been in touch about that thing you requested,' Matthew said.

Anne-Marie waved him away.

'No, seriously. I got caught up with a second investigation, so I've been back at Mount Kosciusko and preparing reports on two different cases.'

Anne-Marie had read about the arrest in the Madeline Bright murder and realised that her small matter of saucy photographs was trivial in the scheme of things and said so to Matthew.

'No, it's not,' he said earnestly. 'I absolutely agree with issuing him a stern warning not to use the images in any way, and I'll get that sorted this week, I promise.'

'It's Christmas, Matthew!'

'Yeah, but I'm not doing much this year, so I'll have plenty of time.'

Before she could think it through, she suddenly found herself inviting him to join them all the next day for Christmas lunch.

'Lou said all orphans are welcome, and that sounds like you too.'

He gave her a heart-melting smile, and she felt that humiliating flush begin again.

CHAPTER 88: LOUISE
Monday 25 December

Louise and Theodore were having five people for Christmas lunch. Anne-Marie, Nina and Matthew would be there, as well as Theodore's sister Mary-Ellen and her husband Clive.

She was busy stuffing the turkey and listening to the seven o'clock radio news bulletin when her phone rang. She quickly wiped her hands to answer it.

'Good morning, Louise? It's Nancy from Huntington Retreat.'

'Oh. Is Chloe all right?' Louise said anxiously, turning down the radio. They hadn't been able to speak with Chloe since she had checked into the Southern Highlands homestead a week ago, but they had received emails every two or three days from Nancy sharing Chloe's progress.

'Actually, that's why I'm calling. Chloe is managing extremely well, and we wondered if you and Theodore would like to pop in for afternoon tea today? Being Christmas and all.'

'Yes!' Louise said at lightning speed. Her eyes danced excitedly. She had been dreading the notion of getting through Christmas day without her beautiful daughter.

'That's great. We will look forward to seeing you both at two.'

Louise rushed upstairs to tell Theodore the good news.

'We'll just enjoy dessert with everyone when we get back,' Theodore said, reassuring her that they should still have everyone over for lunch as planned.

And Louise agreed. It would give her something to focus on now for the next five hours before they headed off. So, she busied herself with the task of finishing stuffing the turkey, glazing the ham and chopping vegetables. When the girls arrived downstairs for breakfast several hours later, she explained the change in plans.

'Why don't we have a Christmas dinner instead?' Nina proposed, but Louise shrugged away her suggestion.

'No. This is perfect because I wasn't sure how I was going to manage sitting at the dining table without Chloe. I would really like you guys to enjoy a lovely, relaxed lunch and we'll see you for Christmas pudding.'

Despite Nina and Anne-Marie's protests, Louise was adamant.

After the food was organised and the kitchen tidied away, they brought fresh coffee into the lounge room to swap Christmas gifts.

Louise received a massage and facial voucher at Canberra's most luxurious day spas from her friends, and she gave each of them a piece of jewellery she had made just for them. A decorative silver ring for Anne-Marie and a slim topaz bracelet for Nina.

****

Louise's nerves were shot as she and Theodore waited patiently in the large courtyard with their cup of tea and mince pie, among a dozen or so other guests. Most looked just like them, worried but excitable parents.

And then suddenly Chloe appeared. Her youthful face beamed at the sight of them both.

After much hugging and tears, Louise finally released her daughter and stood back to let Theodore have his turn.

Chloe's skin was luminous, and her eyes were white and clear. Louise hadn't quite realised the toll that Chloe's unhealthy lifestyle had taken until she looked at her now.

Taking chunks of fruit cake and refreshing their tea, the three of them sat down at one of the small tables.

'How is it all going?' Theodore asked, not yet letting go of Chloe's hand.

'Really good,' Chloe said, surprising them both. 'I know I said I didn't want to come, but now that I'm here, I don't know if I want to leave.' She gave a small laugh, but Louise felt momentarily alarmed at the prospect.

'It's okay, Mum. I'm coming home,' said Chloe, giving Louise a small prod. 'The counsellors and the support group sessions have been so great. I don't feel like such a weirdo idiot anymore.'

'Oh, darling. You were never a weirdo idiot,' Louise said.

'Yeah, but I made some dumb decisions, and I think I would have kept making them if you hadn't brought in the heavy-duty artillery and booked me in here.'

They all shared a laugh.

'Well, it did seem a tad excessive at the time,' Theodore commented, looking at Louise. 'But I'm glad it was the right move.'

'Yeah, me too.' Chloe looked at them both adoringly.

CHAPTER 89: MATTHEW

'Where's Louise?' Matthew had been handed a beer within moments of arriving at Louise and Theodore's house but couldn't see any sign of her.

Anne-Marie explained about the late invitation to visit Chloe and their rush to be with her.

'She insisted we all still enjoy a Chrissy feast here, so cheers,' Anne-Marie said, raising her glass of wine to him and the others on the back deck.

He knew Nina of course and was introduced to Theodore's sister Mary-Ellen and her husband Clive Walton. Both lecturers at the Australian National University, they were easy company, and before long Matthew had discovered some mutual friends and a shared passion for the Canberra Raiders rugby league team.

He was enjoying himself and realised he hadn't felt this relaxed for some time. Especially not at Christmas—usually the most difficult time of the year. It was the season of very little joy in his past life. A time of loss and despair. First the late miscarriage of his son, which happened just two days before Christmas, and then the demise of his marriage on Christmas Eve two years later, when he had swapped his corporate suit for a police badge. But he would never regret changing careers.

The unhappy memories had always been a great motivation to work the Christmas holiday shifts.

But not this year.

He was here, with friends. Well, he thought of Anne-Marie and Nina as friends now, and he had a feeling that Clive and Mary-Ellen could become friends too.

'What are you doing over here on your own?' Anne-Marie asked, finding him looking over the back garden.

'Just realising that it's been a long time since I was doing this on Christmas day,' he said, indicating the beer in his hand and the group on the deck. 'I'm usually at work and Christmas comes and goes without much notice.'

'That sounds a bit tragic!' Anne-Marie teased him, making him laugh at himself.

'Yeah, I sound like a misery guts, sorry about that,' he said shamefacedly.

But she waved him away. 'I do get it though. It's hard, isn't it, when you're single. Christmas, I mean.'

They both stood quietly for a moment, and he could feel their synchronicity.

'All right, guys, let's serve up,' Nina's cheerful voice sounded from the doorway leading on to the deck, and they all went into the kitchen to assemble the food.

The enormous turkey was basted to perfection. The aroma filled the room, and Matthew realised how hungry he was and how long it had been since he had enjoyed a feast like this. The roasted potatoes, pumpkin and onions were transferred to a platter by Clive, whilst Mary-Ellen began slicing the honey-smoked ham.

'What can I do?' He suddenly felt useless as he watched the others work industriously around him.

'Take these out to the table,' Nina said, handing him a large salad bowl and tongs.

It didn't take long for them all to be seated and the food served, and chatter resumed.

Matthew topped up wineglasses and looked around the smiling faces until he found himself lingering on one in particular. Anne-Marie looked radiant, her eyes dancing with excitement as she chatted away. He remembered the moody, unfriendly woman he had met not that long ago and contrasted her with this warm, funny and engaging woman now facing him.

She caught him looking at her and winked as she continued telling a humorous story to Clive whilst Nina and Mary-Ellen talked quietly beside him.

A few hours later as Matthew and Clive sat discussing sport at the table, they heard the front door open. The others were in the kitchen tidying up the dishes, and so Matthew got up to investigate.

Louise and Theodore had arrived home and looked weary and emotional.

After giving Matthew a quick kiss hello, Louise excused herself and went upstairs.

'Louise just needs a moment,' Theodore explained, accepting a glass of red wine from Clive. 'It was wonderful to see Chloe, but bloody tough saying goodbye. Even though it's only for another week.'

The men wandered into the kitchen, where music was blaring from a small portable speaker and the women were immersed in stacking the dishwasher and talking loudly.

'Theodore! You're back,' said Mary-Ellen, moving over to instantly hug her brother. He dismissed her offers to make them up a plate each.

'This will do the trick nicely,' Theodore said, indicating his glass of wine.

'What about Christmas pudding?' Nina suggested.

'Yes, let's have the Christmas pud!' Louise said, materialising with moist eyes and a watery smile. Nina and Anne-Marie took it in turns to hug her.

After wrestling herself free, Louise doused the Christmas pudding in a generous dose of brandy, and Matthew refilled wineglasses.

They then watched as Theodore lit the pudding, the brandy flames leaping dramatically into the sky before simmering down and coating the pudding. In seconds the spectacle was over, and they took their desserts to the deck.

CHAPTER 90: NINA
Thursday 28 December

For three days now Nina had been enjoying lazy days at Louise and Theodore's where the four of them had got into an easy pattern of cohabiting.

Most mornings Anne-Marie met Matthew for a bike ride, and Nina laid out her yoga mat and props for a quiet practice and meditation in the leafy back garden.

Afternoons were a lazier affair with them each swapping sections of the newspaper to read, curling up with a novel or breaking out a board game.

It had been a much-needed reprieve for Nina, following the exhausting sessions she had endured with her accountant and lawyer over the past few weeks and the irrevocable damage to her marriage. David was cooperating with authorities and communicating via his own lawyer. Their house would more than likely need to be sold, but there were worse things in life to endure, she thought, looking over at Louise and Theodore, who were doing their best to keep busy whilst clearly anxious about their daughter.

Chloe was due home on New Year's Eve, and Nina and Anne-Marie would leave that morning. They didn't want to intrude on the family reunion.

Anne-Marie had hinted that she might linger about with Matthew for a few days and cycle the Alpine Way together and camp. Nina and Louise had teased her mercilessly because Anne-Marie and a tent wasn't something they ever expected to see. Sure, Anne-Marie loved nature and adventure but usually with five-star luxury thrown in.

Matthew was breaking down some of their friend's untenable standards and in a good way.

Nina had agreed to attend a New Year's Eve gala at the glamourous Bondi Icebergs restaurant in Sydney, and whilst it was predominantly for work, she was looking forward to getting dressed up again.

The gala was sponsored by Dermott's champagne company, and Sassy Swift would be among the VIP guests, along with a host of other well-known faces including actors, musicians, socialites, influencers and politicians.

'Please come,' had been Dermott's words to her when they last met, just before Christmas.

And perhaps she would.

****

Nina had bought a new silver sequinned shift dress for the party, and now standing in front of the mirror, she realised it looked much shorter than she had remembered. Her stiletto heels seemed to have inched up the hemline, but it was too late to worry about that now.

Her strawberry blonde curls had been carefully styled to hang loosely around her face and shoulders, and she wore twice the amount of make-up as usual. There would be social photographers at the event, and if she was snapped with her star recruit or anyone else for that matter, she wanted to sparkle.

Arriving just after eight, it was the amazing light show that first caught her attention as she walked up to the entrance of the stunning Bondi Icebergs. Tonight it had been transformed from a stylish restaurant to a buzzing nightclub, complete with laser lights beaming to the beat of über cool music and spectacular imagery beamed along the long wall of the inside space.

Accepting a delicious-looking pink cocktail on her way in, she began to look around for familiar faces. She knew more than a few people in the industry and her share of celebrities. In seconds she spotted Sassy, but as she went to make her way towards her, she was intercepted by Dermott.

Wearing a tuxedo, he looked like a James Bond double.

'Wow, look at you!' Dermott said, leaning in to kiss her and standing back to admire her outfit.

'You too,' Nina said.

'I'm glad you decided to come.' He reached to squeeze her hand.

'I am too,' Nina said, smiling back at his intense gaze.

Nina wanted the year ahead to signify a fresh start and a much happier year than the one she was now ending.

CHAPTER 91: ANNE-MARIE

Every preconception that Anne-Marie had about men was flipped on its head with Matthew. The crumpled shirt, three-day growth, beer-drinking policeman was the polar opposite of the sophisticated, wealthy Henry—who she had always assumed was her ideal man.

Why? Where did she get the notion that a clean-cut wealthy professional was the only man she could be with, never a laid-back tradie, let alone a poorly dressed detective?

But the three days they spent together cycling and overnighting in campgrounds along the Alpine Way was the best holiday she had ever had.

Anne-Marie felt energised by the fresh mountain air, stimulated by their diverse conversations about everything from nature and favourite adventures to climate change, and excited by every glance, touch or romantic gesture Matthew made.

On their final night, Matthew suggested they freedom camp instead of setting up at another crowded holiday park, which would be even busier and noisier on New Year's Eve.

They settled on a secluded spot along a river bend, and the picturesque location and peaceful solitude was magical.

They had bought two bottles of champagne, a takeaway roast chicken and eggplant salad, and a block of dark chocolate from the petrol station on their drive.

The night was warm and still as they sat with their small feast and plastic glasses, dangling their feet into the cool water as it made its way down the mountain.

Anne-Marie was just thinking how idyllic it was when Matthew leaned towards her and kissed her.

She pulled back and studied his handsome, tanned features.

'I thought that would never happen,' she said, releasing a breath.

'I was too scared,' he said coyly.

'Scared? You, a big burly detective?' Anne-Marie smirked, but inwardly she understood. She had been unfriendly and hostile to Matthew in their early days, before then firmly placing him in the "Louise's friend" category.

'I think your bark is worse than your bite,' he said, pulling her towards him and kissing her more intensely.

****

Waking at sunrise the next morning, Anne-Marie was momentarily confused where she was until she turned over to see a sleeping Matthew beside her, his naked chest lightly expanding and contracting in his deep slumber. She slipped from under the sleeping bag they had thrown over themselves in the late throes of passion and fetched her discarded clothes nearby.

She was now especially grateful for their isolated hideaway and went down to the river to throw some water on her face and fill the billy for coffee.

'Hey,' Matthew said lazily, watching her walk back up to their camp. He had his jeans on and was just tugging on yesterday's T-shirt.

'I woke up and you were fast asleep,' Anne-Marie said, now feeling self-conscious. She set the billy down on their small burner and played with the knobs for a moment, and when it started, she looked up to see a doting smile across his face.

'Come here,' he whispered, and she could only oblige, falling into his strong arms. Matthew enveloped her body in his before looking down and grazing her lips. They must have kissed for some time because it was the screaming sound of the boiling water that broke them apart.

'That was a pretty good New Year's,' Matthew drawled, filling up the mugs with the steaming liquid.

'Just pretty good?' Anne-Marie raised her eyebrow quizzically, feeling his eyes sizzle.

Laughing, he handed her coffee over but not before kissing her lingeringly once more.

'Can I see you in Sydney?' he asked now, as they sat back at the river with their mugs and last night's uneaten chocolate bar for breakfast.

Why had she never given him the time of day before now? She was glad she had finally come to her senses and gone with her heart, not her head, this time.

'Maybe,' said Anne-Marie cheekily, but deliciously pleased.

The year 2022 was shaping up to be wonderful. Not only had she been offered the role with Ziggy Annear, which would commence in late January, but she now had a gorgeous boyfriend to look forward to as well.

CHAPTER 92: LOUISE
Sunday 31 December

'Happy New Year.' Louise kissed Chloe before wrapping her arms around her precious daughter.

'Happy New Year, Mum,' Chloe said, snuggling in.

Theodore handed over a champagne flute to Louise before filling another glass with non-alcoholic wine for Chloe.

The Sydney nine-o'clock fireworks display had just been broadcast on television, and Louise doubted any of them would still be awake for the midnight ones. The day had taken its toll, although in a good way.

Louise and Theodore had arrived at Huntington Retreat mid-morning for Chloe's exit interview with her therapist, which had been highly emotional. They had learnt of Chloe's escalating experimentation with drugs and alcohol for the past year and a half, especially since she had taken on her job at the club. Wanting to fit in with the older, cooler crowd she had embraced the drug culture.

They were also told of Chloe's emotional struggles. How had they not realised she never felt like she measured up to her mother's artistic prowess and never would or her father's brilliant cleverness? Or her many friends? She had been flailing in dangerous self-doubt and depression.

Louise shed tears at hearing about her daughter's low self-esteem and anxiety and her need to bolster her confidence through self-medicating and indulging in destructive behaviour patterns. Ongoing therapy and anti-depression medication had been prescribed.

Louise hadn't wanted to rush Chloe with too many questions, and so she was surprised when her daughter volunteered her plans as they sat now on the sofa, with the television volume turned low.

'I want to study psychology and be a counsellor,' Chloe said, looking from Louise to Theodore. 'I really want to make a difference in people's lives.'

Theodore gave Louise a smile and nod, as that had answered at least one question Louise had had with regards to what their daughter would do in the year ahead. They were agreed that a second gap year was out of the question. The therapist had said that Chloe would need structure, responsibility and a focus so that she didn't succumb to the patterns of the year they had just had.

'We also found a Narcotics Anonymous youth group for me to join in Dixon,' Chloe said. 'I want to be part of a community, just like I was at Huntington.'

'We hope you will stay on here for a while too,' Theodore suggested tentatively.

'Find your feet?' Louise added, cautiously watching for Chloe's independent streak to flair, but instead her daughter replied that she would like that.

'Plus I'll be a poor student, don't forget.' Chloe had laughed.

'Well, there's always a shift for you at the shop?'

'I'd like that,' Chloe said, biting her lip and looking on the brink of tears.

'I'd like that too,' Louise said, hugging her daughter close.

ACKNOWLEDGEMENTS

I would like to thank my husband Peter for championing my writing journey. A fellow artist (musician), he has been a constant source of love and encouragement.

Thank you to my family and friends for assisting in the production of this book – from the story development to proofreading. I would like to especially thank dear friend John Davidson, for his generous assistance in shaping the criminal procedures and processes in this story, and any mistakes are of my own making. Special mentions also go to Penny Hunstead, Sandy Allen, CA Larmer and Simone Larmer for reading early copies of this manuscript and providing crucial input.

Writing this book feels like it has been a team effort, and I truly appreciate everyone who has shared helpful suggestions, inspiring words and taken the time to read my novels.

ABOUT THE AUTHOR

Michelle Larmer was born and raised in Port
Moresby, Papua New Guinea and lives in Sydney,
Australia with her husband. She is a former regional
television journalist and today splits her time between
working in public relations and fiction writing.
Other books written by Michelle include
The Plantation, her debut novel.